"The collection offers a wide ranging look at the Washington scene, reflecting the author's own observations as a *Washington Post* reporter . . . Ward Just is an admirer of Ernest Hemingway and there is something of the tone of Hemingway in these stories."
—*New York Times*

Also by Ward Just

Jack Gance
The American Ambassador
Stringer

The
CONGRESSMAN WHO LOVED FLAUBERT
Ward Just

Carroll & Graf Publishers, Inc.
New York

First Carroll & Graf edition 1990

Carroll & Graf Publishers, Inc.
260 Fifth Avenue
New York, NY 10001

ISBN: 0-88184-587-6

Manufactured in the United States of America

For
Geoffrey and Priscilla Wolff

A Note

THE characters in these stories are imaginary. They are not based on persons living or dead. Nor are the situations *à clef*. The author is obliged to state this clearly, in view of the tendency of "the new journalism" to blend fact and fiction.

There is one other reason. Journalism is useful, but truth wears many masks and in Washington facts sometimes tend to mislead. All the facts sometimes tend to mislead absolutely.

W. J.
Washington, D.C.

Contents

The Congressman
Who Loved Flaubert

THE deputation was there: twelve men in his outer office and he would have to see them. His own fault, if "fault" was the word. They'd called every day for a week, trying to arrange an appointment. Finally his assistant, Annette, put it to him: Please see them. Do it for me. Wein is an old friend, she'd said. It meant a lot to Wein to get his group before a congressman whose name was known, whose words had weight. LaRuth stood and stretched; his long arms reached for the ceiling. He was his statuesque best that day: dark suit, dark tie, white shirt, black beard neatly trimmed. No jewelry of any kind. He rang his secretary and told her to show them in, to give them thirty minutes, and then ring again; the committee meeting was at eleven.

"What do they look like?"

"Scientists," she said. "They look just as you'd expect scientists to look. They're all thin. And none of them are smoking." LaRuth laughed. "They're pretty intense, Lou."

"Well, let's get on with it."

He met them at the door, as they shyly filed in. Wein and his committee were scientists against imperialism. They were physicists, biologists, linguists, and philosophers. They introduced themselves, and LaRuth wondered again what it was that a philosopher did in these times. It had to be a grim year for philosophy. The introductions done, LaRuth leaned back, a long leg hooked over the arm of his chair, and told them to go ahead.

They had prepared a congressional resolution, a sense-of-the-Congress resolution, which they wanted LaRuth to introduce. It was a message denouncing imperialism, and as LaRuth read it he was impressed by its eloquence. They had assembled hard facts: so many tons of bombs dropped in Indochina, so many "facilities" built in Africa, so many American soldiers based in Europe, so many billions in corporate investment in Latin America. It was an excellent statement, not windy as so many of them are. He finished reading it and turned to Wein.

"Congressman, we believe this is a matter of simple morality. Decency, if you will. There are parallels elsewhere, the most compelling being the extermination of American Indians. Try not to look on the war and the bombing from the perspective of a Westerner looking East but of an Easterner facing West." LaRuth nodded. He recognized that it was the war that truly interested them. "The only place the analogy breaks down is that the Communists in Asia appear to be a good deal more resourceful and resilient than the Indians in America. Perhaps that is because there are so many more of them." Wein paused to smile. "But it is genocide either way. It is a stain on the American Congress not to raise a specific voice of protest, not only in Asia but in the other places where American policy is doing violence . . ."

LaRuth wondered if they knew the mechanics of moving a congressional resolution. They probably did; there was no need for a civics lecture. Wein was looking at him, waiting for a response. An intervention. "It's a very fine statement," LaRuth said.

"Everybody says that. And then they tell us to get the signatures and come back. We think this ought to be undertaken from the inside. In that way, when and if the resolution is passed, it will have more force. We think that a member of Congress should get out front on it."

An admirable toughness there, LaRuth thought. If he were Wein, that would be just about the way he'd put it.

"We've all the people you'd expect us to have." Very rapidly, Wein ticked off two dozen names, the regular antiwar contingent on the Democratic left. "What we need to move with this is not the traditional dove, but a more moderate man. A moderate man with a conscience." Wein smiled.

"Yes," LaRuth said.

"Someone like you."

LaRuth was silent a moment, then spoke rapidly. "My position is this. I'm not a member of the Foreign Affairs Committee or the Appropriations Committee or Armed Services or any of the others where . . . war legislation or defense matters are considered. I'm not involved in foreign relations, I'm in education. It's the Education and Labor Committee. No particular reason why those two subjects should be linked, but they are." LaRuth smiled. "That's Congress for you."

"It seems to us, Congressman, that the war — the leading edge of imperialism and violence — is tied to everything. Education is a mess because of the war. So is labor. And so forth. It's all part of the war. Avoid the war and you avoid all the other problems. The damn thing is like the Spanish

Inquisition, if you lived in Torquemada's time, fifteenth-century Spain. If you did try to avoid it you were either a coward or a fool. That is meant respectfully."

"Well, it is nicely put. Respectfully."

"But you won't do it."

La Ruth shook his head. "You get more names, and I'll think about cosponsoring. But I won't front for it. I'm trying to pass an education bill right now. I can't get out front on the war, too. Important as it is. Eloquent as you are. There are other men in this House who can do the job better than I can."

"We're disappointed," Wein said.

"I could make you a long, impressive speech." His eyes took in the others, sitting in chilly silence. "I could list all the reasons. But you know what they are, and it wouldn't do either of us any good. I wish you success."

"Spare us any more successes," Wein said. "Everyone wishes us success, but no one helps. We're like the troops in the trenches. The Administration tells them to go out and win the war. You five hundred thousand American boys, you teach the dirty Commies a lesson. Storm the hill, the Administration says. But the Administration is far away from the shooting. We're right behind you, they say. Safe in Washington."

"I don't deny it," LaRuth said mildly.

"I think there are special places in hell reserved for those who see the truth but will not act." LaRuth stiffened, but stayed silent. "These people are worse than the ones who love the war. You are more dangerous than the generals in the Pentagon, who at least are doing what they believe in. It is because of people like you that we are where we are."

Never justify, never explain, LaRuth thought; it was pointless anyway. They were pleased to think of him as a war criminal. A picture of a lurching tumbrel in Pennsylvania Avenue flashed through his mind and was gone, an oddly comical image. LaRuth touched his beard and sat upright. "I'm sorry you feel that way. It isn't true, you know." One more number like that one, he thought suddenly, and he'd throw the lot of them out of his office.

But Wein would not let go. "We're beyond subtle distinctions, Mr. LaRuth. That is one of the delightful perceptions that the war has brought us. We can mumble all day. You can tell me about your responsibilities and your effectiveness, and how you don't want to damage it. You can talk politics and I can talk morals. But I took moral philosophy in college. An interesting academic exercise." LaRuth nodded; Wein was no fool. "Is it true you wrote your Ph.D. thesis on Flaubert?"

"I wrote it at the Sorbonne," LaRuth replied. "But that was almost twenty years ago. Before politics." LaRuth wanted to give them something to hang on to. They would appreciate the irony, and then they could see him as a fallen angel, a victim of the process; it was more interesting than seeing him as a war criminal.

"Well, it figures."

LaRuth was surprised. He turned to Wein. "How does it figure?"

"Flaubert was just as pessimistic and cynical as you are."

LaRuth had thirty minutes to review his presentation to the committee. This was the most important vote in his twelve years in Congress, a measure which, if they could steer it through the House, would release a billion dollars over three years' time to elementary schools throughout the country. The measure was based on a hellishly complicated formula which several legal experts regarded as unconstitutional; but one expert is always opposed by another when a billion dollars is involved. LaRuth had to nurse along the chairman, a volatile personality, a natural skeptic. Today he had to put his presentation in exquisite balance, giving here, taking there, assuring the committee that the Constitution would be observed, and that all regions would share equally.

It was not something that could be understood in a university, but LaRuth's twelve years in the House of Representatives would be justified if he could pass this bill. Twelve years, through three Presidents. He'd avoided philosophy and concentrated on detail, his own time in a third-rate grade school in a southern mill town never far from his mind: that was the reference point. Not often that a man was privileged to witness the methodical destruction of children before the age of thirteen, before they had encountered genuinely soulless and terrible events: the war, for one. His bill would begin the process of revivifying education. It was one billion dollars' worth of life, and he'd see to it that some of the money leaked down to his own school. LaRuth was lucky, an escapee on scholarships, first to Tulane and then to Paris, his world widened beyond measure; Flaubert gave him a taste for politics. *Madame Bovary* and *A Sentimental Education* were political novels, or so he'd argued at the Sorbonne; politics was nothing more or less than an understanding of ambition, and the moral and social conditions that produced it in its various forms. The House of Representatives: *un stade des arrivistes*. And now the press talked him up as a southern liberal, and the northern Democrats came to him for help. Sometimes he gave it, sometimes he didn't. They could not understand the refusals — Lou, you won with sixty-five percent of the vote the last time out. What do you want, a coronation? They were critical that he would not get out front on the war and would not vote against bills vital to southern interests. (Whatever they were, now that the entire region was dominated by industrial combines whose headquarters were in New York or Chicago — and how's that for imperialism, Herr Wein?) They didn't, or couldn't, grasp the paper-thin depth of his support. The Birchers and the segs were everywhere, and each time he voted with the liberals in the House he'd hear from a few of them. *You are being watched.* He preferred a low silhouette. All those big liberals didn't understand that a man with enough money could still buy an election in his district; he told them that LaRuth compromised was better than no LaRuth at all. That line had worked well the first four or five years he'd been in Washington; it worked no longer. In these times, caution and realism were the refuge of a scoundrel.

The war, so remote in its details, poisoned everything. He read about it every day, and through a friend on the Foreign Affairs Committee saw some classified material. But he could not truly engage himself in it, because he hadn't seen it firsthand. He did not know it intimately. It was clear enough that it was a bad war, everyone knew that; but knowing it and feeling it were two different things. The year before, he'd worked to promote a junket, a special subcommittee to investigate foreign aid expenditures for education. There was plenty of scandalous rumor to justify the investigation. He tried to promote it in order to get a look at the place firsthand, on the ground. He wanted to look at the faces and the villages, to see the countryside which had been destroyed by the war, to observe the actual manner in which the war was being fought. But the chairman refused, he wanted no part of it; scandal or no scandal, it was not part of the committee's business. So the trip never happened. What the congressman knew about the war he read in newspapers and magazines and saw on television. But that did not help. LaRuth had done time as an infantryman in Korea and knew what killing was about; the box did not make it as horrible as it was. The box romanticized it, cleansed it of pain; one more false detail. Even the blood deceived, coming up pink and pretty on the television set. One night he spent half of Cronkite fiddling with the color knob to get a perfect red, to insist the blood look like *blood*.

More: Early in his congressional career, LaRuth took pains to explain his positions. He wanted his constituents to know what he was doing and why, and two newsletters went out before the leader of his state's delegation took him aside one day in the hall. Huge arms around his shoulders, a whispered conference. Christ, you are going to get killed, the man said. *Don't do that.* Don't get yourself down on paper on every raggedy-ass bill that comes before Congress. It makes you a few friends, who don't remember, and a lot of enemies, who do. Particularly in your district: you are way ahead of those people in a lot of areas, but don't advertise it. You've a fine future here; don't ruin it before you've begun. LaRuth thought the advice was captious and irresponsible and disregarded it. And very nearly lost reelection, after some indiscretions to a newspaperman. *That* son of a bitch, who violated every rule of confidence held sacred in the House of Representatives.

His telephone rang. The secretary said it was Annette.

"How did it go?" Her voice was low, cautious.

"Like a dream," he said. "And thanks lots. I'm up there with the generals as a war criminal. They think I make lampshades in my spare time."

Coolly: "I take it you refused to help them."

"You take it right."

"They're very good people. Bill Wein is one of the most distinguished botanists in the country."

"Yes, he speaks very well. A sincere, intelligent, dedicated provocateur. Got off some very nice lines, at least one reference to Dante. A special place in hell is reserved for people like me, who are worse than army generals."

"Well, that's one point of view."

"You know, I'm tired of arguing about the war. If Wein is so goddamned concerned about the war and the corruption of the American system, then why doesn't he give up the fat government contracts at that think tank he works for —"

"That's unfair, Lou!"

"Why do they think that anyone who deals in the real world is an automatic sellout? Creep. A resolution like that one, *even if passed*, would have no effect. Zero effect. It would not be binding, the thing's too vague. They'd sit up there and everyone would have a good gooey warm feeling, *and nothing would happen*. It's meaningless, except of

course for the virtue. Virtue everywhere. Virtue trium-
phant. So I am supposed to put my neck on the line for
something that's meaningless —" LaRuth realized he was
near shouting, so he lowered his voice. "Meaningless," he
said.

"You're so hostile," she said angrily. "Filled with hate.
Contempt. Why do you hate everybody? You should've
done what Wein wanted you to do."

He counted to five and was calm now, reasonable. His
congressional baritone: "It's always helpful to have your
political advice, Annette. Very helpful. I value it. Too bad
you're not a politician yourself." She said nothing, he could
hear her breathing. "I'll see you later," he said, and hung
up.

LaRuth left his office, bound for the committee room.
He'd gone off the handle and was not sorry. But sometimes
he indulged in just a bit too much introspection and self-justi-
fication, endemic diseases in politicians. There were certain
basic facts: his constituency supported the war, at the same
time permitting him to oppose it so long as he did it quietly
and in such a way that "the boys" were supported. Oppose
the war, support the troops. A high-wire act — very Flau-
bertian, that situation; it put him in the absurd position of
voting for military appropriations and speaking out against
the war. Sorry, Annette; that's the way we think on Capitol Hill. It's a question of what you *vote* for. Forget the
fancy words and phrases, it's a question of votes. Up,
down, or "present." Vote against the appropriations and
sly opponents at home would accuse him of "tying the

hands" of American troops and thereby comforting the enemy. Blood on his fingers.

2

LARUTH was forty; he had been in the House since the age of twenty-eight. Some of his colleagues had been there before he was born, moving now around the halls and the committee rooms as if they were extensions of antebellum county courthouses. They smelled of tobacco and whiskey and old wool, their faces dry as parchment. LaRuth was amused to watch them on the floor; they behaved as they would at a board meeting of a family business, attentive if they felt like it, disruptive if their mood was playful. They were forgiven; it was a question of age. The House was filled with old men, and its atmosphere was one of very great age. Deference was a way of life. LaRuth recalled a friend who aspired to a position of leadership. They put him through his paces, and for some reason he did not measure up; the friend was told he'd have to wait, it was not yet time. He'd been there eighteen years and was only fifty-two. Fifty-two! Jack Kennedy was President at forty-three, and Thomas Jefferson had written the preamble when under thirty-five. But then, as one of the senior men put it, this particular fifty-two-year-old man had none of the durable qualities of Kennedy or Jefferson. That is, he did not have Kennedy's money or Jefferson's brains. Not that money counted for very much in the House of Representatives; plutocrats belonged in the other body.

It was not a place for lost causes. There were too many

conflicting interests, too much confusion, too many turns to the labyrinth. Too many *people:* four hundred and thirty-five representatives and about a quarter of them quite bright. Quite bright enough and knowledgeable enough to strangle embarrassing proposals and take revenge as well. Everyone was threatened if the eccentrics got out of hand. The political coloration of the eccentric didn't matter. This was one reason why it was so difficult to build an ideological record in the House. A man with ideology was wise to leave it before reaching a position of influence, because by then he'd mastered the art of compromise, which had nothing to do with dogma or public acts of conscience. It had to do with simple effectiveness, the tact and strength with which a man dealt with legislation, inside committees, behind closed doors. That was where the work got done, and the credit passed around.

LaRuth, at forty, was on a knife's edge. Another two years and he'd be a man of influence, and therefore ineligible for any politics outside the House — or not ineligible, but shopworn, no longer new, no longer fresh. He would be ill-suited, and there were other practical considerations as well, because who wanted to be a servant for twelve or fourteen years and then surrender an opportunity to be master? Not LaRuth. So the time for temporizing was nearly past. If he was going to forsake the House and reach for the Senate (a glamorous possibility), he had to do it soon.

LaRuth's closest friend in Congress was a man about his own age from a neighboring state. They'd come to the Hill in the same year, and for a time enjoyed publicity in the national press, where they could least afford it. *Two Young Liberals from the South*, that sort of thing. Winston was then a bachelor, too, and for the first few years they shared a house in Cleveland Park. But it was awkward, there were too many women in and out of the place, and one groggy morning Winston had come upon LaRuth and a friend taking a shower together and that had torn it. They flipped for the house and LaRuth won, and Winston moved to grander quarters in Georgetown. They saw each other frequently and laughed together about the curiosities of the American political system; Winston, a gentleman farmer from the plantation South, was a ranking member of the House Foreign Affairs Committee. The friendship was complicated because they were occasional rivals: who would represent the New South? They took to kidding each other's press notices: LaRuth was the "attractive liberal," Winston the "wealthy liberal." Thus, LaRuth became Liberal Lou and Winston was Wealthy Warren. To the extent that either of them had a national reputation, they were in the same category: they voted their consciences, but were not incautious.

It was natural for Wein and his committee of scientists to go directly to Winston after leaving LaRuth. The inevitable telephone call came the next day, Winston inviting LaRuth by for a drink around six; "small problem to discuss." Since leaving Cleveland Park, Warren Winston's life had become plump and graceful. Politically secure now, he had sold his big house back home and bought a small jewel of a place on Dumbarton Avenue, three bedrooms and a patio in back, a mirrored bar, and a sauna in the basement. Winston was drinking a gin and tonic by the

pool when LaRuth walked in. The place was more elegant
than he'd remembered; the patio was now decorated with
tiny boxbushes and a magnolia tree was in full cry.

They joked a bit, laughing over the new southern mani-
festo floating around the floor of the House. They were
trying to find a way to spike it without seeming to spike it.
Winston mentioned the "small problem" after about thirty
minutes of small talk.

"Lou, do you know a guy named Wein?"

"He's a friend of Annette's."

"He was in to see you, then."

"Yeah."

"And?"

"We didn't see eye to eye."

"You're being tight-lipped, Liberal Lou."

"I told him to piss off," LaRuth said. "He called me a
war criminal, and then he called me a cynic. A pessimist, a
cynic, and a war criminal. All this for some cream-puff
resolution that will keep them damp in Cambridge and
won't change a goddamed thing."

"You think it's *that* bad."

"Worse, maybe."

"I'm not sure. Not sure at all."

"Warren, *Christ*."

"Look, doesn't it make any sense at all to get the position of the House on record? That can't fail to have some
effect downtown, and it can't fail to have an effect in the
country. It probably doesn't stand a chance of being
passed, but the effort will cause some commotion. The
coon'll be treed. Some attention paid. It's a good thing to
get on the record, and I can see some points being made."

"What points? Where?"

"The newspapers, the box. Other places. It'd show that at least some of us are not content with things as they are. That we want to change . . ."

LaRuth listened carefully. It was obvious to him that Winston was trying out a speech; like a new suit of clothes, he took it out and tried it on, asking his friend about the color, the fit, the cut of it.

". . . the idea that change can come from within the system . . ."

"Aaaaaoh," LaRuth groaned.

"No?" Innocently.

"How about, *and so, my fellow Americans, ask not what you can do for Wein, but what Wein can do for you.* That thing is loose as a hound dog's tongue. Now tell me the true gen."

"Bettger's retiring."

"You don't say." LaRuth was surprised. Bettger was the state's senior senator, a living southern legend.

"Cancer. No one knows about it. He'll announce retirement at the end of the month. It's my only chance for the next four years, maybe *ever*. There'll be half a dozen guys in the primary, but my chances are good. If I'm going to go for the Senate, it's got to be now. This thing of Wein's is a possible vehicle. I say possible. One way in. People want a national politician as a senator. It's not enough to've been a good congressman, or even a good governor. You need something more: when people see your face on the box they want to think *senatorial,* somehow. You don't agree?"

LaRuth was careful now. Winston was saying many of

the things he himself had said. Of course he was right, a senator needed a national gloss. The old bulls didn't need it, but they were operating from a different tradition, pushing different buttons. But if you were a young man running statewide for the first time, you needed a different base. Out there in television land were all those followers without leaders. People were pulled by different strings now. The point was to identify which strings pulled strongest.

"I think Wein's crowd is a mistake. That resolution is a mistake. They'll kill you at home if you put your name to that thing."

"No, Lou. You do it a different way. With a little rewording, that resolution becomes a whole lot less scary; it becomes something straight out of Robert A. Taft. You e-*liminate* the fancy words and phrases. You steer *clear* of words like 'corrupt' or 'genocide' or 'violence.' You and I, Lou, we know: our people *like* violence, it's part of our way of life. So you don't talk about violence, you talk about American traditions, like 'the American tradition of independence and individuality. Noninterference!' Now you are saying a couple of *other* things, when you're saying that, Lou. You dig? That's the way you get at imperialism. You don't call it imperialism because that word's got a bad sound. A foreign sound."

LaRuth laughed. Winston had it figured out. He had to get Wein to agree to the changes, but that should present no problem. Wealthy Warren was a persuasive man.

"Point is, I've got to look to people down there like I can make a difference . . ."

"I think you've just said the magic words."

"Like it?"

"I think so. Yeah, I think I do."

"*To make the difference. Winston for Senator.* A double line on the billboards, like this." Winston described two lines with his finger and mulled the slogan again. "*To make the difference. Winston for Senator.* See, it doesn't matter what kind of difference. All people know is that they're fed up to the teeth. *Fed up and mad at the way things are.* And they've got to believe that if they vote for you, in some unspecified way things will get better. Now I think the line about interference can do double duty. People are tired of being hassled, in all ways. Indochina, down home." Winston was a gifted mimic, and now he adopted a toothless expression and hooked his thumbs into imaginary galluses. "Ah think Ah'll vote for that-there Winston. Prob'ly won't do any harm. Mot do some good. Mot mek a diff'rence."

"Shit, Warren."

"You give me a little help?"

"Sure."

"Sign the Wein thing?"

LaRuth thought a moment. "No," he said.

"What the hell, Lou? Why not? If it's rearranged the way I said. Look, Wein will be out of it. It'll be strictly a congressional thing."

"It doesn't mean anything."

"Means a whole lot to me."

"Well, that's different. That's political."

"If you went in too, it'd look a safer bet."

"All there'd be out of that is more gold-dust-twins copy. You don't want that."

"No, it'd be made clear that I'm managing it. I'm out front. I make all the statements, you're back in the woodwork. Far from harm's way, Lou." Winston took his glass and refilled it with gin and tonic. He carefully cut a lime and squeezed it into the glass. Winston looked the part, no doubt about that. Athlete's build, big, with sandy hair beginning to thin; he could pass for an astronaut.

"You've got to find some new names for the statement."

"Right on, brother. Too many Jews, too many foreigners. Why are there no scientists named Robert E. Lee or Thomas Jefferson? Talmadge, Bilbo." Winston sighed and answered his own question. "The decline of the WASP. Look, Lou. The statement will be forgotten in six weeks, and that's fine with me. I just need it for a little national coverage at the beginning. Hell, it's not decisive. But it could make a difference."

"You're going to *open* the campaign with the statement?"

"You bet. Considerably revised. It'd be a help, Lou, if you'd go along. It would give them a chance to crank out some updated New South pieces. The networks would be giving that a run just as I announce for the Senate and my campaign begins. See, it's a natural. Bettger is Old South, I'm New. But we're friends and neighbors, and that's a fact. It gives them a dozen pegs to hang it on, and those bastards love *you*, with the black suits and the beard and that cracker accent. It's a natural, and it would mean a hell of a lot, a couple of minutes on national right at the beginning. I wouldn't forget it. I'd owe you a favor."

LaRuth was always startled by Winston's extensive knowledge of the press. He spoke of "pieces" and "pegs," A.M. and P.M. cycles, facts "cranked out" or "folded in," who was up and who was down at CBS, who was analyzing Congress for the editorial board of the *Washington Post*. Warren Winston was always accessible, good for a quote, day or night; and he was visible in Georgetown.

"Can you think about it by the end of the week?"

"Sure," LaRuth said.

He returned to the Hill, knowing that he thought better in his office. When there was any serious thinking to be done, he did it there, and often stayed late, after midnight. He'd mix a drink at the small bar in his office and work. Sometimes Annette stayed with him, sometimes not. When LaRuth walked into his office she was still there, catching up, she said; but she knew he'd been with Winston.

"He's going to run for the Senate," LaRuth said.

"Warren?"

"That's what he says. He's going to front for Wein as well. That statement of Wein's — Warren's going to sign it. Wants me to sign it, too."

"Why you?"

"United front. It would help him out. No doubt about that. But it's a bad statement. Something tells me not to do it."

"Are you as mad as you look?"

He glanced at her and laughed. "Does it show?"

"To me it shows."

It was true; there was no way to avoid competition in politics. Politics was a matter of measurements, luck, and

ambition, and he and Warren had run as an entry for so
long that it disconcerted him to think of Senator Winston;
Winston up one rung on the ladder. He was irritated that
Winston had made the first move and made it effortlessly.
It had nothing to do with his own career, but suddenly he
felt a shadow on the future. Winston had seized the day all
right, and the fact of it depressed him. His friend was
clever and self-assured in his movements; he took risks; he
relished the public part of politics. Winston was expert at
delivering memorable speeches on the floor of the House;
they were evidence of passion. For Winston, there was no
confusion between the private and the public; it was all
one. LaRuth thought that he had broadened and deepened
in twelve years in the House, a man of realism, but not
really a part of the apparatus. Now Winston had stolen the
march, he was a decisive step ahead.

LaRuth may have made a mistake. He liked and understood the legislative process, transactions which were only
briefly political. That is, they were not public. If a man
kept himself straight at home, he could do what he liked in
the House. So LaRuth had become a fixture in his district,
announcing election plans every two years from the front
porch of his family's small farmhouse, where he was born,
where his mother lived still. The house was filled with political memorabilia; the parlor walls resembled huge bul-
letin boards, with framed photographs, testimonials, parch-
ments, diplomas. His mother was so proud. His life seemed
to vindicate her own, his successes hers; she'd told him so.
His position in the U.S. Congress was precious, and not
lightly discarded. The cold age of the place had given him

a distrust of anything spectacular or . . . capricious. The House: no place for lost causes.

Annette was looking at him, hands on hips, smiling sardonically. He'd taken off his coat and was now in shirtsleeves. She told him lightly that he shouldn't feel badly, that if *he* ran for the Senate he'd have to shave off his beard. Buy new clothes. Become prolix, and professionally optimistic. But, as a purchase on the future, his signature . . .

"Might. Might not," he said.

"Why not?"

"I've never done that here."

"Are you refusing to sign because you don't want to, or because you're piqued at Warren? I mean, Senator Winston."

He looked at her. "A little of both."

"Well, that's foolish. You ought to sort out your motives."

"That can come later. That's my business."

"No. Warren's going to want to know why you're not down the line with him. You're pretty good friends. He's going to want to know *why*."

"It's taken me twelve years to build what credit I've got in this place. I'm trusted. The Speaker trusts me. The chairman trusts me."

"Little children see you on the street. Gloryosky! There goes trustworthy Lou LaRuth —"

"Attractive, liberal," he said, laughing. "Well, it's true. This resolution, if it ever gets that far, is a ball-buster. It could distract the House for a month and revive the whole issue. Because it's been quiet we've been able to get on with our work, I mean the serious business. Not to get pompous about it."

"War's pretty important," she said.

"Well, is it now? You tell me how important it is." He put his drink on the desk blotter and loomed over her. "Better yet, you tell me how this resolution will solve the problem. God forbid there should be any solutions, though. Moral commitments. Statements. Resolutions. They're the great things, aren't they? Fuck solutions." Thoroughly angry now, he turned away and filled the glasses. He put some ice and whiskey in hers and a premixed martini in his own.

"What harm would it do?"

"Divert a lot of energy. Big play to the galleries for a week or two. Until everyone got tired. The statement itself? No harm at all. Good statement, well done. No harm, unless you consider perpetuating an illusion some kind of harm."

"A lot of people live by illusions, *and what's wrong with getting this House on record?*"

"But it won't be gotten on record. That's the point. The thing will be killed. It'll just make everybody nervous and divide the place more than it's divided already."

"I'd think about it," she said.

"Yeah, I will. I'll tell you something. I'll probably end up signing the goddamned thing. It'll do Warren some good. Then I'll do what I can to see that it's buried, although God knows we won't lack for gravediggers. And then go back to my own work on the school bill."

"I think that's better." She smiled. "One call, by the

way. The chairman. He wants you to call first thing in the
morning."

"What did he say it's about?"

"The school bill, dear."

Oh shit, LaRuth thought.

"There's a snag," she said.

"Did he say what it was?"

"I don't think he wants to vote for it anymore."

3

WINSTON was after him, trying to force a commitment,
but LaRuth was preoccupied with the school bill, which
was becoming unstuck. It was one of the unpredictable
things that happen; there was no explanation for it. But
the atmosphere had subtly changed and support was evap-
orating. The members wavered, the chairman was suddenly
morose and uncertain; he thought it might be better to
delay. LaRuth convinced him that was an unwise course
and set about repairing damage. This was plumbing, pure
and simple; talking with members, speaking to their fears.
LaRuth called it negative advocacy, but it often worked.
Between conferences a few days later, LaRuth found time
to see a high-school history class, students from his alma
mater. They were touring Washington and wanted to talk
to him about Congress. The teacher, sloe-eyed, stringy-
haired, twenty-five, wanted to talk about the war; the students were indifferent. They crowded into his outer office,
thirty of them; the secretaries stood aside, amused, as the
teacher opened the conversation with a long preface on
the role of the House, most of it inaccurate. Then she

asked LaRuth about the war. What was the congressional role in the war?

"Not enough," LaRuth replied, and went on in some detail, addressing the students.

"Why not a congressional resolution demanding an end to this terrible, immoral war?" the teacher demanded. "Congressman, why can't the House of Representatives take matters into its own hands?"

"Because" — LaRuth was icy, at once angry, tired, and bored — "because a majority of the members of this House do not want to lose Asia to the Communists. Irrelevant, perhaps. You may think it is a bad argument. I think it is a bad argument. But it is the way the members feel."

"But why can't that be *tested?* In votes."

The students came reluctantly awake and were listening with little flickers of interest. The teacher was obviously a favorite, their mod pedagogue. LaRuth was watching a girl in the back of the room. She resembled the girls he'd known at home, short-haired, light summer dress, full-bodied; it was a body that would soon go heavy. He abruptly steered the conversation to his school bill, winding into it, giving them a stump speech, some flavor of home. He felt the students with him for a minute or two, then they drifted away. In five minutes they were somewhere else altogether. He said good-bye to them then and shook their hands on the way out. The short-haired girl lingered a minute; she was the last one to go.

"It would be good if you could do something about the war," she said.

"Well, I've explained."

"My brother was killed there."

LaRuth closed his eyes for a second and stood without speaking.

"Any gesture at all," she said.

"Gestures." He shook his head sadly. "They never do any good."

"Well," she said. "Thank you for your time." LaRuth thought her very grown-up, a well-spoken girl. She stood in the doorway, very pretty. The others had moved off down the hall; he could hear the teacher's high whine.

"How old was he?"

"Nineteen," she said. "Would've been twenty next birthday."

"Where?"

"They said it was an airplane."

"I'm so sorry."

"You wrote us a letter, don't you remember?"

"I don't know your name," LaRuth said gently.

"Ecker," she said. "My brother's name was Howard."

"I remember," he said. "It was . . . some time ago."

"Late last year," she said, looking at him.

"Yes, that would be just about it. I'm very sorry."

"So am I," she said, smiling brightly. Then she walked off to join the rest of her class. LaRuth stood in the doorway a moment, feeling the eyes of his secretary on his back. It had happened before; the South seemed to bear the brunt of the war. He'd written more than two hundred letters, to the families of poor boys, black and white. The deaths were disproportionate, poor to rich, black to white, South to North. Oh well, he thought. Oh hell. He walked back into his office and called Winston and told him he'd go along. In a limited way. For a limited period.

Later in the day, Winston called him back. He wanted LaRuth to be completely informed, and up-to-date.

"It's rolling," Winston said.

"Have you talked to Wein?"

"I've talked to Wein."

"And what did Wein say?"

"Wein agrees to the revisions."

"Complaining?"

"The contrary. Wein sees himself as the spearhead of a great national movement. He sees scientists moving into political positions, cockpits of influence. His conscience is as clear as rainwater. He is very damp."

LaRuth laughed; it was a private joke.

"Wein is damp in Cambridge, then."

"I think that is a fair statement, Uncle Lou."

"How wonderful for him."

"He was pleased that you are with us. He said he misjudged you. He offers apologies. He fears he was a speck . . . harsh."

"Bully for Wein."

"I told everyone that you would be on board. I knew that when the chips were down you would not fail. I knew that you would examine your conscience and your heart and determine where the truth lay. I knew you would not be cynical or pessimistic. I know you want to see your old friend in the Senate."

They were laughing together. Winston was in one of his dry, mordant moods. He was very salty. He rattled off a dozen names and cited the sources of each member's conscience: money and influence. "But to be fair — always be fair, Liberal Lou — there are a dozen more who are doing it because they want to do it. They think it's *right*."

"*Faute de mieux*."

"I am not schooled in the French language, Louis. You are always flinging French at me."

"It means, 'in the absence of anything better.' "

Winston grinned, then shrugged. LaRuth was depressed, the shadow lengthened, became darker.

"I've set up a press conference, a half dozen of us. All moderate men. Men of science, men of government. I'll be out front, doing all the talking. OK?"

"Sure." LaRuth was thinking about his school bill.

"It's going to be jim-dandy."

"Swell. But I want to see the statement beforehand, music man."

Winston smiled broadly and spread his hands wide. Your friendly neighborhood legislator, concealing nothing; merely your average, open, honest fellow trying to do the right thing, trying to do his level best. "But of course," Winston said.

Some politicians have it; most don't. Winston has it, a fabulous sense of timing. Everything in politics is timing. For a fortnight, the resolution dominates congressional reportage. "An idea whose time has come," coinciding with a coup in Latin America and a surge of fighting in Indochina. The leadership is agitated, but forced to adopt a conciliatory line; the doves are in war paint. Winston appears regularly on the television evening news. There are hearings before the Foreign Affairs Committee, and these

produce pictures and newsprint. Winston, a sober legislator, intones *feet to the fire.* There are flattering articles
in the newsmagazines, and editorial support from the major
newspapers, including the most influential paper in Winston's state. He and LaRuth are to appear on the cover of
Life, but the cover is scrapped at the last minute. Amazing
to LaRuth, the mail from his district runs about even. An
old woman, a woman his mother has known for years,
writes to tell him that he should run for President. Incred-
ible, really: the Junior Chamber of Commerce composes
a certificate of appreciation, commending his enterprise
and spirit, "an example of the indestructible moral fiber
of America." When the networks and the newspapers cannot find Winston, they fasten on LaRuth. He becomes
something of a celebrity, and wary as a man entering dark-
ness from daylight. He tailors his remarks in such a way
as to force questions about his school bill. He finds his
words have effect, although this is measurable in no definite
way. His older colleagues are amused; they needle him
gently about his new blue shirts.

He projects well on television, his appearance is striking;
his great height, the black suits, the beard. So low-voiced,
modest, diffident; no hysteria or hyperbole (an intuitive reporter would grasp that he has contempt for "the Winston
Resolution," but intuition is in short supply). When an
interviewer mentions his reticent manner, LaRuth smiles
and says that he is not modest or diffident, he is pessimistic.
But his mother is ecstatic. His secretary looks on him with
new respect. Annette thinks he is one in a million.

No harm done. The resolution is redrafted into harmless
form and is permitted to languish. The language incompre-

hensible, at the end it becomes an umbrella under which anyone could huddle. Wein is disillusioned, the media looks elsewhere for its news, and LaRuth returns to the House Education and Labor Committee. The work is backed up; the school bill has lost its momentum. One month of work lost, and now LaRuth is forced to redouble his energies. He speaks often of challenge and commitment. At length the bill is cleared from committee and forwarded to the floor of the House, where it is passed; many members vote aye as a favor, either to LaRuth or to the chairman. The chairman is quite good about it, burying his reservations, grumbling a little, but going along. The bill has been, in the climactic phrase of the newspapers, watered down. The three years are now five. The billion is reduced to five hundred million. Amendments are written, and they are mostly restrictive. But the bill is better than nothing. The President signs it in formal ceremony, LaRuth at his elbow. The thing is now law.

The congressman, contemplating all of it, is both angry and sad. He has been a legislator too long to draw obvious morals, even if they were there to be drawn. He thinks that everything in his life is meant to end in irony and contradiction. LaRuth, at forty, has no secret answers. Nor any illusions. The House of Representatives is no simple place, neither innocent nor straightforward. Appearances there are as appearances elsewhere: deceptive. One is entitled to remain fastidious as to detail, realistic in approach.

Congratulations followed. In his hour of maximum triumph, the author of a law, LaRuth resolved to stay inside the belly of the whale, to become neither distracted nor moved. Of the world outside, he was weary and finally unconvinced. He knew who he was. He'd stick with what he had and take comfort from a favorite line, a passage toward the end of *Madame Bovary*. It was a description of a minor character, and the line had stuck with him, lodged in the back of his head. Seductive and attractive, in a pessimistic way. *He grew thin, his figure became taller, his face took on a saddened look that made it nearly interesting.*

Nora

NORA believed that my stories were old-fashioned. She said once, "Friend, why don't you write something up-to-date, immediate. The romantics are dead. Friend, they're *gone.*" She was really very serious about it, and I had to tell her that hers was a liverish idea whose time had not yet come. Not that it made any difference, because in 1965 nobody would buy the stories except an obscure review in the Midwest, whose payment was in prestige. In the first six months of 1965 I had two payments of prestige with a third on the way. For eats, as Nora liked to call them, I worked as a researcher for *Congressional Weekly Digest,* an expensive private newsletter which purported to give its subscribers advance information on legislation pending before the House and Senate. I was paid a hundred dollars a week for reading the *Congressional Record* and reporting my findings to the editor, who would rearrange them into breathless verbless sentences.

But that had little to do with Nora Bryant. She was English and had come to Washington as correspondent for one of the popular London dailies. She had good looks, and good brains to go with the good looks, but she was admired for her idiosyncrasies. Nora believed that America was alive and Britain was dead; interesting, amusing in its way, but dead nonetheless. She thought that this country was open to possibilities and in perpetual motion in a way that Britain was not. She had a wide circle of American friends, and spent as little time at the British embassy as she could manage; the ambassador there was an aging peer whom she called the kandy-kolored tangerine-flake stream-lined baron. In a bewitching West Riding accent she spoke American slang, and the effect was hilarious: Somerset Maugham imitating Allen Ginsberg. Her specialty was southern politicians and she told me it was a high point of her life here when she spent an evening with the then-occupant of the White House and came away with enough vocabulary to last her a month or more. She came to my apartment after dinner at the White House, still laughing over all the wonderful words and phrases she'd learned. I tried to pump her about the man himself, what he was like. How much did he drink? What was on his mind? Was his mood hot or cold?

"I didn't have a thermometer up his bum, friend," she said.

"Come on, Nora! Give! What did he say about the war? Anything about —"

She laughed and shook her head.

"Nora . . ."

"That dog won't hunt," she said, and that was that.

We'd met at a party on Capitol Hill, and I was quickly taken with her because she asked me about my stories. Under any normal circumstance a writer doesn't like to be asked what he's working on, except in Washington no one cared at all. No one ever asked me about my fiction, so my identity was frozen at "researcher for *Congressional*

Weekly Digest," a job I despised and was defensive about. Nora understood right away. She was persistent in asking about the stories and it was clear to me as I answered her that I hadn't thought them out clearly. She saw this, too, but did not press it. She told me to keep working, and everything would be fine.

"You'll be jake," she said. "You're a writer, I can see that."

"Oh? Just how?"

"You don't know what you think."

Nora is barely five feet tall, and I come in at just under six feet four. In a brief moment of anger I saw her as a little girl who worked for a second-string London newspaper, looking up at me and figuratively patting me on my head; the patronage was unmistakable and outrageous, but I was charmed. At our first meeting, listening to her voice and watching her glide around the room, I fell half in love with her. She seemed wonderfully cheerful and inquisitive, intelligent and sure of herself, and I liked the attention. It was a large, jumbled party and she left it early, and two days later called me at my apartment.

"I've got a pretty good tip," she said. "Will that do you any good at that thing you work for? That newsletter?" She sounded brisk and impatient.

"Sure," I said. Gottschault, the editor, paid me a ten-dollar bonus for any authentic inside story, anything that had not been printed elsewhere. I had never taken advantage of this, because I seldom read the newspapers and therefore did not know what was news and what wasn't.

"All right," she said. "The Senate Finance Committee will take up the oil section of the tax bill on Thursday.

They will report it on Friday. There will be one day of discussion, in private. No more."

"Thursday, huh?"

"Yes, Thursday. Now does that suggest anything to you?"

"No," I said.

"Well, today is Wednesday. That might suggest to you that the oil section *has already been written.*"

"Stop the presses," I said.

"Would you like to have that? For your very own?"

"Are you under the Official Secrets Act?"

"I'll send it over by messenger."

"Are you serious?" I suspected a joke.

"Yes," she said, and rang off.

The document arrived that afternoon, and when I gave it to Gottschault he whooped with pleasure and literally did stop the presses to get it in the newsletter. Then he gave me a twenty-dollar bonus, but when I asked Nora to dinner to celebrate, she declined.

I don't remember when she started calling me "friend." It was probably the period when she began dropping in at my apartment unannounced. This was a two-room apartment in a brownstone off Connecticut Avenue. I'd know she was there when I heard the phonograph; Brahms if she was in a good mood, Bunk Johnson if she was not. She'd taken to American jazz along with everything else and loved to listen to the blues when she was low. I worked in my bedroom and would finish whatever passage I was writing and join her and we'd sit and talk, sometimes all night. Washington politicians fascinated her, she thought they had nothing in common with the ones she knew in Britain. She came to modify that opinion, but in the first months in Washington she was as intrigued as a biologist investigating a new species. Nora developed categories for the politicians that she met.

It was clear from the first month that there would be no romance. I was never exactly sure why. She seemed to want a friend, someone off the Washington political circuit, who was compatible and what she called "talkable." I was pleased and flattered — romance or no — because I was being very reclusive and difficult at that time of my life, and Nora was one of the ornaments of Washington. She had her own center of gravity, a distinct and (I thought) hard-won personal style. Late at night we tried to analyze the town, what made it work, why some men were successful and others were not, why women seemed to fail, and what each had to do with the other.

A couple of times a month she'd give me a document or memcon — she'd picked up government slang, a "memcon" is a memorandum of conversation — and as a result of that I was a boon to Gottschault. Now he was paying me a hundred and twenty-five dollars a week, plus a thirty-dollar bonus for really important items. Items that were exclusive. Because of Nora's tips, Gottschault had become very popular at the National Press Club bar. It was clear to everyone that he had inside information, "inside skinny," as Nora called it. I enjoyed the extra money, but more than that I enjoyed Nora. I'd wait for her unannounced visits, when we'd sit and drink coffee or beer and talk. The longer she stayed in Washington, the more doubts she had about America; but she never regretted leaving London. Of course she was by then one of the best-known foreign correspondents in town. Her copy was nothing much to read because of the form in which she was obliged to write. The editor of her paper had a theory that no paragraph should be longer than two sentences, no sentence longer than ten words, and no word longer than three syllables. Once she wrote a two-hundred-word political story entirely in haiku, but her foreign desk mixed up the paragraphing so it came out wrong. But it was a noble effort, and (as a matter of fact) excellent haiku.

It was partly Nora's encouragement that gained me my first real sale, a story to the *Saturday Evening Post* for eight hundred dollars. I'd received word in the morning and immediately rang her up at her office. But she'd gone. I was agitated the rest of the day, because I wanted to share this news with her. I'd been working on fiction for two years and this was the first evidence I had that I could sell my stories for money. I felt wonderful and spent most of the day congratulating myself that I hadn't "cheated" or "lowered my standards" or pandered to "the popular taste." I had eight hundred dollars and virtue, too. At four in the afternoon, I heard the phonograph. Bunk Johnson.

I opened the bedroom door right away and saw Nora sitting on the couch. It had taken me four months to write the story, Nora had followed it from the beginning. I trusted her absolutely, and now I looked at her and grinned and told her I'd sold the story and mentioned the amount. She knew everything about it, including how difficult the writing had been. I was certain that with this story behind me, I'd fly. "Nora, it's really going to move now. The bastards can't ignore me any longer," I said, and scooped her up in my arms. She was so tiny and light it was like lifting a doll. She put her arms around my neck and kissed me on the cheek. She was crying, and I began to laugh.

"Oh, come on. No tears. Think of this, a real sale. Money. I've the letter right here. They really like it. They're thinking of putting my name on the cover of the magazine. Do you know how many copies they sell a week? Five or six million copies." I held her tightly and laughed. "Every dentist in America reads the *Saturday Evening Post*."

When I put her down she was still crying. I started to say something funny, but understood then that the tears had nothing to do with me or the magazine. There was something frightening to me about Nora in tears, Nora hurt with no visible wounds. She cried without covering her eyes.

She stopped crying after a minute, and I went into the kitchen and made tea. She was sitting quietly in the middle of the sofa, a bleak look on her face, her hands in her lap, listening to Bunk Johnson. We had become very close over the six months, and I had a strong protective instinct toward her; it was partly fatherly, and strongly sexual. She had been the one encouraging me, and now I wanted to help her. I thought she was too strong to be hurt that badly by anyone.

"Do you want to talk?"

She shook her head.

"Drink your tea," I said.

She held the cup in both hands, sipping the tea.

"Trouble," she said.

"A man?"

She nodded, yes.

She was involved with someone, and I knew it was serious. She was the only woman in Washington who took sex seriously enough to be private about it. She had her own standards, which were uninhibited and seemed to me healthy; she said she loved the pleasure that sex gave her and never confused that with anything else. Beyond that, she was discreet. From time to time she stayed at my apartment, although we never slept together; different stars, wrong chemistry, she said. Those nights she was usually in flight from a bore or a sponge. She was cheerful about it, acknowledging that sometimes she picked the wrong man, and vice versa. But Nora's life was not an open book.

"Well, I'm a mess today."

I wanted desperately to say the right thing. She had always encouraged me when I needed encouragement, and I felt very much in her debt. I knew right away that this had something to do with her current liaison, the details of which I knew practically nothing.

"You tell me what you want to tell me," I said, as gently as I could.

"I have to write a story this afternoon."

"Well, I'll write the story. You tell me what it's about, and I'll write it. Then you can rest for a bit and tell me what you want to tell me later."

She smiled at that: "Friend, you can't write a story for my paper. You don't know how, your sentences are too long. Won't work."

"I'll cable London and tell them that you've got the flu."

"Would you do that?"

"Of course."

"No need to cable, just call Judson." Judson was the bureau chief, the man she worked for.

I telephoned, Judson was out, so I left word with the answering service. Then I went to Nora, who was stretched out full-length on the couch. It took an hour to get the essentials out of her, but I still didn't have the man's name. It didn't matter to me who he was, except from one or two things she said I gathered he was someone important. She told me the usual things, what he was like, what they talked about, how they'd met, what he meant to her, and how it was ended. It was "permanent," she said, but ended. He wanted to get a divorce from his wife, and that was the last — definitely the last — thing she wanted. It would ruin his career, and he would be no good at anything else. She would become an ego doctor, and she wanted no part of that; she saw it as martyrdom and it seemed to her wrong. If you're an architect or a lawyer and you get into trouble you can resign and go practice somewhere else. If you're a politician and get into trouble, that's the end of it.

"I can't see him as anything else, and I don't want to see him as anything else. I don't care a hoot in hell," she said. "Getting married doesn't mean anything to me. It never did. I don't care about it. He gets his . . . juice from politics. Politics and me. If politics goes, there's only me. You know what happens then." She shook her head. "It's a disaster."

"Does he know the way you feel?"

"Yes, and he says it doesn't matter what I feel."

"Doesn't *matter?*"

"Yes, he says it matters to him. 'The only way,' he says. 'The only decent way.' Besides, he hates his wife."

"Oh."

"He says he doesn't want to go on sleeping with me in motel rooms." She smiled wanly. "Well, that's rather sweet, really."

"I guess it is."

"The thing is, he's really an awfully good politician. I mean . . . he's really *good*. Damned good. You know?"

"Look, Nora. Who is he?"

"You don't know?" She was incredulous.

"How would I know?"

"I thought everybody knew."

"Maybe everybody does. I don't."

When she told me, I shook my head. I'd had no idea.

He was a midwestern senator, about forty, one of those who is always named on the lists of Most Effective Legislators, and for the last two elections as one of the many vice-presidential possibilities. As senators go in Washington, he had what the press calls high visibility. He was not a member of the leadership, but he had an independent base of his own, particularly among academics. He had been a university president at twenty-eight and resigned to run for the Senate. That was a highly implausible sequence except that this particular university president's father had been governor, and his brother now published the state's largest newspaper. That was all I knew about him, except that he was a Washington politician who was clean. He was intelligent, he was not a thief, and he seemed to know his own mind.

Nora stayed with me three days, she barely moved from the sofa. Her spirits improved, her confidence returned. In the mornings we drank coffee, in the afternoons tea, and in the evenings beer. She told me the story of the romance, how he had enchanted her . . .

"I mean literally enchanted," she said. Then she went on to list the things they did together, her tone of voice changing. She became wistful, a most un-Nora tone of voice. She talked of the future, too, how he'd plotted his political career, the plans he had for the next national convention; this was before he decided to divorce his wife. But she thought he had a self-destructive part of him, and that was not always unappealing, surrounded as he was by success.

And not once in the first weeks did they ever speak of politics. They spent a weekend together in Nova Scotia, "and this was in December. Gosh, friend, did you ever spend a weekend in December in Nova *Scotia?* I was touched, he used my name to register at the hotel. Mr. and Mrs. N. Bryant. The way he did it, he was . . . oh, I don't know what he was doing. I took it to mean he regarded us as equals. We spent that time in Nova Scotia, and other weekends in other wonderful places. Have you ever been to Chincoteague Island? And all the time he was legislating in the Senate, and passing me the documents, the bad ones, to get them out in the open." She laughed. "He used to call me his publisher. He loved to see them all in print, then listen to the bitching and moaning inside the committee. The FBI was called in to investigate the leak. I thought it was all obvious, too obvious, so I passed some of the stuff on to you. Didn't you ever wonder where it came from?"

"Well, I thought you just picked it up . . ."

"Friend, you don't just 'pick up' the sort of stuff I was passing on to you. It was all golden." She smiled proudly. "He loved it, really loved doing it, watching the reaction . . ."

"The romance, Nora. It sounds to me a little heavy, it isn't the sort of thing you pursue in motel rooms."

"But it is! Why not? It was just fine, it was going along just fine. Nothing wrong, he'd have to go home from time to time. But his wife didn't really care. I mean he was under no pressure. Not from her. Not from me. Now it's ended."

"Say again why."

"He'd be ruined without his political life. I *know that*. What do we do now? Does he open a law office, become a lobbyist? How about a beachcomber?"

"My God, you can get a divorce and still run for office. A hell of a lot of guys do that. You can divorce, remarry, and run for office. There's no law . . ."

"You don't understand. He's a Catholic. He wants to marry me. You don't recover from that. Not in his state. No, he'd have to give up politics altogether. Go do something else."

"You've talked it all out?"

"Until I'm out of breath! He won't listen. He wants to wait a year or two, then marry. He says he's through with motels and through with his wife. But he doesn't know what I know. Which is that without politics he's a different man, and not as good a man. It's the self-destructive part."

"Nora, someone isn't defined entirely by what they do. People have other sides to them, sides that have nothing to do with . . . plumbing or writing or politics."

"Not him," she said.

"So you've refused absolutely to marry him."

She nodded slowly.

"What did he say?"

"He said he was going to get the divorce anyway."

"And then?"

"And then I'll change my mind, he said."

The next day Nora left, sad but in control. She was talking now about going back to England or cajoling her editor into a long assignment abroad, Africa or the Far East. She told me that she would never, never marry the man; it would destroy both their spirits, they'd be hypnotized for the rest of their lives by what he'd thrown away. She knew in her heart it was irretrievable. She said she understood the political mind too well not to understand that. If a man gives up power against his will it haunts him. And there was no need, she said. No need at all. Just before she left my apartment she made the only anti-American remark I'd ever heard from her. She generally regarded this country with great affection and enthusiasm, and it amused her to write pro-American articles for her Yankee-baiting London newspaper.

"Goddamned American innocence," she said. "Destructive virtue."

"Thank you, Graham Greene," I replied. The remark

irritated me, it was unjustified; it was true of course, but unjustified. "Can't you see your man is in a bind, too?"

"Well, we're all in a bind. But he's the one who's forcing it, *and there's no need*."

I couldn't quarrel with that.

A week later, she called me for a favor. She said she would ask me the favor if I would cook her dinner. We ate a memorable meal, and she was full of praise for the *Saturday Evening Post* story and one other story I was working on. All the time she was talking, I was looking at her and wishing the stars and chemistry had been right. She was in good form, looking as beautiful as I'd ever seen her. She'd had another of her dinners at the White House and was full of new stories and phrases. She was pouring coffee when she said she needed the favor right away.

"He's coming over here tonight," she said.

"Great," I said.

"Just for an hour or two. It's better to talk here, was what I thought. Not that there's very much to talk about. Can you make yourself scarce?"

I smiled at the Americanism. "Sure."

"He's due in about ten minutes."

"I'll go now."

"You can come back in an hour."

"I'll make it an hour and a half."

"I appreciate it. Friend."

"Just keep the door closed, and I'll know you're still here if I get back too early."

So I left, half-angry, half-sad. There was a bar down the street that had a color television set. I hadn't been in the bar in six weeks, but it was empty as usual and I took a seat at the far end, backed up against the wall, and drank draft beer for two hours. I thought I had better give them all the time they needed. While I sat and drank beer I thought about Nora and how she would handle it. It occurred to me that there were a hundred jobs in Washington that the senator could get, all of them close to the — what did they call it? — "the center of events." There were jobs in this town other than elective ones. Editing newsletters. Influence peddling. I began to think of him as an undersecretary of state or an assistant secretary of defense. Depending, of course, on how messy the divorce was. Whether or not the press picked it up. Well. No adulterers in the Pentagon. But as I sat and drank the beer, I understood that the speculations didn't matter. What mattered was Nora, and how she saw it. She'd staked out her territory and was a very determined woman. She loved him, so she understood him, and she understood Washington, too; that was the essence of it. It seemed to me that the way she had constructed her argument made retreat impossible.

The night baseball game ended, and I was alone in the bar. The barman and I were watching the late news. There was film from Saigon and a report on the West Coast dock strike. We were chatting quietly, and then the barman moved off to serve a late arrival who had taken a table in the rear. I was preparing to go, when I caught the last of a sentence from the television announcer: ". . . the senator and his wife had been married for fourteen years." There was no more, but I knew they were talking about Nora's man. I turned to go and saw him then, at the table in the rear of the room, near the color television set. He was staring into his drink, a stricken look on his face. He hadn't taken off his overcoat, its khaki collar concealed his cheeks and jaw. He was almost as big as I am, hunched over the table in the overcoat, his hat on the chair beside him. He stared at the drink and clicked the ice with his finger, apparently unconscious of the surroundings. I turned back to the bar and in a moment I left, leaving a five-dollar bill and walking straight out the door.

I ran up the street to the brownstone, let myself in, and sprinted up the stairs to the second floor. The door was partly ajar, and I could hear Bunk Johnson's blues inside. Nora was sitting on the couch, a drink in front of her, staring at the bookshelves.

"He's gone now," she said. She waited a moment, concentrating, then went on. "He made an announcement tonight; he and his wife are separating. He prepared an announcement, a press release. He and his staff. Is that what you do in Washington? If you decide to get a divorce, leave someone's bed, do you first prepare an announcement to give to the newspapers? Before you've packed, said good-bye?"

"If you're a senator, I guess you do."

"Television, too, I suppose."

"I guess so. I heard it on the news ten minutes ago."

"I suppose you'd want the largest possible distribution, no part of America ignorant of any personal fact. Do you suppose he'll have a briefing for the wire services? Off the record? Deep background, perhaps. Lindley Rule with a release date?" She'd begun to cry.

"Nora, Nora."

"No need," she said.

"Well, *he* thought there was."

"Yes, he did. He did he did he did."

"How was he when he left?"

"He didn't like it," she said.

"It isn't the worst thing I've ever heard a man do."

"No, not the worst. Unless you regard futility as an offense. Or ignoring other people's feelings. Or your own ... your own sense of yourself. To destroy a part of yourself, what you are, what you have, in obedience . . . to some stupid ..."

I wanted to say something to shock her. "How can you be so goddamned sure?"

It was then that she made the remark about romantics dead and dying, although as I look back on it now, that can be taken two ways. In any case, the senator was duly divorced, and Nora got her assignment abroad. I didn't see her again for six years, when I was in London on a holiday and rang her up and we had lunch at the Ritz. It was an elegant lunch, and we talked about everything but that. I was waiting for her to bring up the subject and I suppose she was waiting for me. But there was nothing to be said about it, at that late date. Nothing useful or illuminating or constructive. But I could never tell her, then or later, that I'd seen him that night in the bar, hunched over the table, staring at the glass, clicking the ice cubes with his fingernail. In light of everything since, she'd been right as rain.

Slayton

ALL marriages have private jokes; mine has just one. The joke is Sylvia. When my wife and I have stayed late over the chessboard, or become hypnotized by the late show on the television, we will leave the debris of the evening and go to bed with the words, "Sylvia can clean up in the morning." On the rare occasions when we have guests, we insist that they not worry about the dinner dishes. "Sylvia will take care of it." Of course there is no Sylvia. There never was.

*   *   *

I have breakfasted on coffee, two coddled eggs, and the newspaper, and now I am waiting on the corner for my ride. I look at my watch; Jack Fowler is late. Today I am the fourth man, and Jack drives a Volkswagen. I will be in the rear seat with my legs cramped, squeezed like an orange next to Bill Day. Jack will be talking football with Gershen. A thirty-minute ride to Langley, stop-start, stop-start. I close my eyes, I doze; it is Monday and I think of my vacation, two weeks away. Presently, Bill nudges me and I awaken and see the guard through the window. My ID is in my hand, and I press it against the glass. The guard looks at it and nods. The car moves through the gate, up the road, and into the underground parking lot.

*   *   *

It is a routine day, until three in the afternoon. My secretary brings me a cable, covered by the familiar black-bordered folder.

TOP SECRET

(this is a cover sheet)
Basic Security Requirements
Are Contained In AR 380-5

THE UNAUTHORIZED DISCLOSURE OF THE INFORMATION CONTAINED IN THE ATTACHED DOCUMENT(S) COULD BE PREJUDICIAL TO THE DEFENSE INTERESTS OF THE UNITED STATES.

The U.S. government is careful, thorough. There is a parenthesis at the bottom of the sheet: "(This cover sheet is unclassified when separated from classified documents.)"

*   *   *

I have read the cable, and now I am thinking about it. It is one of the things that fascinates me about my work. I have not been in the field for fifteen years, and all I know is what I read. I see nothing firsthand; my objectivity is complete. And as my superiors have reason to know, my judgments are accurate. I have learned to distinguish good cables from bad, and the writer of this cable is quite nimble, a man with a sure grasp of government form. The paragraphs descend down the page, numbered one to twenty-three. But it is a puzzling cable, and I read it three times. Now I am drinking a cup of tea, waiting for the telephone to ring. I have already told my secretary to call Jack

Fowler to tell him not to wait, and my wife to tell her I will not be home for dinner.

* * *

There are six of us in the conference room; the deputy director, one of his assistants, an area chief and one of his assistants (that is me), and two spear carriers, strangers. We are very anxious to keep this inside the agency. The deputy director: "This is our affair. It has nothing to do with Defense or State or anyone else. We will handle it in-house on a closed basis. This meeting is being held at the request of the director." He does not say what is obvious, that it is a confidential meeting, no written record. Then we talk about Slayton.

* * *

I am wrong about the other two. They are not spear carriers at all, but two of Slayton's close friends. I have read their cables for years but am meeting them face-to-face for the first time. We have generally worked different countries. It is typical of the agency that they should bring these two into this meeting, although they are both outside the chain of command in this matter; strictly speaking, they should not be involved at all. They are part of the old agency, very — what was the word we used to use? — la-di-da. Good schools, rich wives. History majors from Yale, bored lawyers from Wall Street. It's changed now, and we favor mathematicians from UCLA or the University of Chicago. In the general conversation before we get under way, I notice that the blue-eyed one has a southern accent; Virginia, I think. I remember one of his cables that I read years ago. It was from Warsaw, Prague, someplace like that, some Cradle of Western Civilization Enduring the

Long Night of Soviet Communism. It read like an honors thesis, and the last line made me laugh. "Such, anyway, is the melancholy prospect from . . ." The old-boy net at the agency was great for melancholy prospects.

*   *   *

We have all read the same Top Secret cable, from Slayton's Number Two in N——. His nerves show a little in the language, and it takes him a hundred words to get to the point: he thinks that Slayton is having a nervous breakdown. He recommends an immediate replacement. You have to be inside a large bureaucracy to understand the delicacy of this undertaking. The Number Two is running considerable risk, unless he can make his case stick and stick fast. I am reserving my voice, for the moment.

*   *   *

There are several unspokens, for this after all is Slayton. Wonderful Slayton, battered Slayton, Slayton-the-widower, Slayton-the-linguist, protean Slayton. Slayton and his private income. But Slayton has been under very heavy pressure for two years. He has been on station for three, longer than is either usual or desirable. He had — has — excellent contacts and speaks the language. Oh, fluently. And has the credentials.

The embassy has been bombed twice, and Slayton is on all the blacklists. Blacklisted Slayton. Eighteen months ago he was infected with hepatitis, which laid him up for ten weeks. The deputy director wanted to remove him then, but Slayton pleaded to be kept on. It was an elegant cable. Removing him from N——, Slayton told the deputy director, would be *coitus interruptus*. Worse, it would jeopardize the operation. The two were old friends, and the remark gained a certain celebrity around the shop — I mean among those who had access to the cable. It was very highly classified. The DD bent the rules, and Slayton stayed. Now, according to his Number Two, he was bats.

*   *   *

It requires felicity to talk about a man's personal life in a cable. There is no satisfactory way to put it in government language. *Subject was observed drinking twenty-two scotch-and-sodas in the Palace Hotel bar, then was seen to pitch and fall into a lamppost on Ledra Street, where a native seized and made off with his briefcase containing the ciphers.* . . . No, no. So there are code words, and I do not mean of the five-numeral variety. These are the words: eccentric behavior, slurred speech, abnormal working hours, and the most damning of all: "A frequent loss of control." The phrase "erratic personal life" meant a sexual irregularity of some kind.

*   *   *

This meeting is a strange one. It is odd that it was called at all. The normal procedure, in matters of this kind, is for the Number Two (or whomever) to call the DD on a secure line, tell him the facts face-to-face, or voice-to-voice, and get a third party on the scene to make an evaluation. Naturally, if it is a chief of station faulting his deputy or anyone under his command, his word alone is sufficient. The man is removed. But a deputy breaking dishes on his boss is something else. Normally, an independent evaluation is ordered. A station chief does not live in a vacuum: his behavior is known to the ambassador, among others; the chief of the military mission, if any; and there are a number of discreet ways, even in a very large organization, to monitor a man's performance. These devices are built-in. But in N—— the U.S. government has no ambassador, and since the bombing, no embassy. The military mission is small and the colonel in charge of it incompetent. There is a consulate, staffed by three frightened Foreign Service officers. None of these is suitable, and only *in extremis* would we call on an outside agency in a matter of this kind; I cannot recall a time when it was ever done. At any event, in N—— there is only Slayton and his Two and six others scattered around the country. Still, it would have been simple for the Two to telephone. But a cable is more efficient. In a cable, words have weight.

*   *   *

I am not expected to say anything. I am at the meeting because I am the officer assigned to country N—— in Washington. My immediate superior is the area director. He will wait for a signal from the DD before he speaks, and then he will be cautious. Not that it matters at all; I knew what I would do the moment I read the cable. *Get him out*, I said to myself. Right away.

The area director is asked to assess Slayton's performance from this end. He says: "Objectively excellent, although as we all know, he has a tendency to operate on his own overmuch. He is the only officer at that rank in the agency who speaks the language, and writes it. His contacts in N—— are wide and varied. He has shown unusual discretion. In two matters" — he looks at the DD, and at the two strangers — "of great delicacy Slayton performed superbly. One of them went haywire, but that had nothing to do with him." The DD nods, and the area director continues. "A quality man. If it were not for this cable" — he

picks up the paper, holds it a second, and lets it fall —
"there would be no question in my mind about Slayton's
suitability. Of course, he would have been withdrawn next
month anyway. I would not keep a man in a station like
that for more than three years in any case. Not for any
reason." I smile. It is the first time I've heard that.

*   *   *

The deputy director has turned now to the "friends."
He lifts his eyebrows: "Charley?" This is the blue-eyed
one, the older of the two. He lights a cigarette and looks at
his colleague. Now they will close ranks. "I can't believe
it," he says, speaking directly to the DD. "I saw Slayton
two months ago in Rome, and he was fine. He said he'd re-
covered from the hepatitis and was enjoying his tour in
N——. As much as you *can* enjoy N——, which is not a
garden spot, as we all know. He was with one of his daugh-
ters in Rome. I think she lives with his brother. I ran into
him by accident at the . . . circus." Blue-eyes smiles, looking at the DD; the DD returns it. Some private joke. "We
had a drink later; he laughed about drinking Vichy and
soda. He looked very fit, although he'd lost some weight.
With his record . . ." Blue-eyes trails off for a moment, as
if looking for words. "We know his C.V. France during
the war, then Eastern Europe, Hungary, Japan, Cairo, back
to Eastern Europe" — he smiles at the euphemism and
slides on — "the tour at Bragg, and now out there. A vol-
unteered second tour. *Coitus interruptus.*" The DD smiles;
the area director smiles; the two friends smile. "This is not
a man to let an operation go out of control. We know that
from the past. What the hell, this agency is Slayton's life.
In view of what I gather is a certain urgency . . ." The

words come out, *gyathuh's a suht'n uhj'ncy.* "Well, the record . . ." Blue-eyes' voice is soft, persuasive. "I'd trust him with anything," he says.

*   *   *

We are silent, waiting for the DD. "Is it possible the whole thing is an act?"

"It's possible," I said. I did not add that it was not likely. In twenty years in this work I have never heard of a man faking a nervous breakdown. For obvious reasons.

"How well known is he in N——?" This, from the area director.

"Well known," I said. Stupid question. Any man who is station chief for three years in a country like that becomes known. He is probably better known than the foreign minister. It is impossible to be unknown. Also unwise. If they know who you are, they know where to go with their information. I mean the friendlies.

"If this is an act, would he tell his Two?"

"Be very foolish if he didn't," I said.

"Be very foolish if he *did*," Blue-eyes cut in. "No reason to. He couldn't've suspected that his Two would try to break dishes on him." He nodded at the DD: yes, certainly that was it. That was the explanation. "It's a setup," Blue-eyes said.

I looked at him. "Why?"

"You would know that better than I," he drawled. This was not a man to go beyond what he knew, or was supposed to know.

"On the other hand, Slayton's been out there too damned long," the DD said. "The operation is too important to be entrusted to a man who is possibly . . ." The DD shook his head. "I don't understand why the Two waited until the last bloody minute to send his cable. I assume there was a good reason. Also a reason why he did not call. But a thing like this doesn't come out of the blue, not usually."

"Well, he's been accused," Blue-eyes said. "There's no proof."

"The Number Two is an excellent man," the area director said mildly. I waited for the qualification. "Though of course a younger man."

"He's under forty," I said dryly.

"There is no plausible reason for the Two to undercut Slayton. If what he says is false, that will become obvious straightaway. I find it bewildering. Of course, now there is no way to get a third man into the country. There is no way to *know*, and I have been unable to raise the Two on the radiophone." He looked at his watch. "As of just now communications will go *kaput*. Except, of course, our own X-communications. Which are not of much use if no one is there manning the radio." The DD pursed his lips.

"I'd stick," Blue-eyes said, and his friend nodded.

"The only alternative is to put the Two in charge. I wouldn't like to do that, in a situation of this delicacy. Slayton's kept his plans very close." The DD glanced over at the area director, who was staring bleakly at the table. Blue-eyes and his friend were smiling ever so slightly.

*   *   *

Blue-eyes had mentioned "a certain urgency." What that was about was this: Slayton was managing a coup, all by himself. It was known in the cables as Rampart Street; that was the operational code word. Doubtless it had some special meaning for Slayton and his cronies. In this particular coup there was meant to be no American participation at all. Zero. Entirely indigenous, as we say. Three years ago, a half-dozen young army officers approached Slayton, and the plans proceeded from there. Of course, there was no way for my bureau to know all the details, because Slayton did not let us in on his plans; I mean the area director and myself. Slayton made his reports verbally — I suppose there are pieces of paper somewhere — to the director and his deputy. He did not go through channels; he was too old-boy net for that. So those of us here who had the responsibility did not have all the facts. Slayton ignored my messages demanding more information. He fobbed them off on his Two and had enough personal clout with the DD to get away with it. The agency was very excited because Slayton had seemingly squared all the circles. All the negotiations and planning he did himself, personally. Not that there was much of either; all the rebels apparently wanted was Slayton's neutrality.

At any event, he did manage to import Swedish weapons: I heard the DD refer to that in an admiring way one day; yet it was my bureau that found the weapons, that paid for them and arranged for delivery in S——. There were one or two other items of that kind. But officially, the agency was not involved in Rampart Street, and if it succeeded, we were way ahead; if it failed, we'd lost nothing. That is, Slayton lost nothing. Those of us here would lose a great deal. For we would be asked to pay the price for an operation in which we had no more than nominal control. That is a fact of life: when there is a failure, someone must pay up. The thing would leak; it always did, sooner or later. So that is what Slayton had been doing in

N—— for three years, and it was the consensus within the agency that no one could put it together except Slayton. Slayton had the finesse. That was the "certain urgency" about the meeting now, because the coup was supposed to get under way today. Or would if Slayton were sane.

* * *

The DD has gone through all of Slayton's personal files and finds nothing to suggest imbalance. *Au contraire*, the print-out indicates unusual stability. A photo accompanies the file. I see a middle-aged, red-headed man, scowling. A bit fleshy, standing in a slouch, a cigarette holder in his left hand. I look at the picture upside down: Slayton is quite mad, no doubt about it. Blue-eyes and his friend have long since been excused, and it is just the four of us now. The DD goes around the table, requesting recommendations. The truth of the matter is that he has no options, at this late date; he had them this morning, but he does not have them now. He must go with Slayton or abandon the game altogether.

* * *

I am in my office now, drinking a cup of tea and waiting for the first cables. I have asked my secretary to stay, and she is in the outer office, waiting as I am. We have heard nothing from the Two since his cable this morning. I have a bad feeling about this operation, a feeling that it will fail. The psychology has gone wrong, as it sometimes does in the middle of a chess game; the atmosphere darkens, and you know you are going to lose, although you do not see how or why. I am ashamed to admit that I almost hope it does. It will teach them a lesson: field men cannot be entrusted with operational control. They are too close, they lose their perspective; it is a question of limited parameter. That is a fact of life. If you surrender control, you surrender responsibility. What is the value of an area director or a bureau chief if he is not permitted to control operations in his zone of responsibility? It is pointless not to use the resources of the agency. What is the point of the apparatus here if it is not used? It is not entirely my problem, because I have been here for twenty years and I will be here for twenty more, and the situation *is* improving. It is better than it was, thanks largely to the computers. They have simplified some of the problems. There are only a few Slaytons left. There are fewer of them every year.

*   *   *

The cable from the Two finally arrived, brief, too brief. It turned out more or less as I expected. Slayton did have a breakdown, and the coup did fail, although there is some difference of opinion here as to what "fail" means in this case. Slayton is now in a private hospital in S——, and the Two is on leave. We were lucky to get them out of the country at all, particularly Slayton, who was completely haywire. It was done this way: with a show of compassionate concern, the White House ordered army medical teams to N—— to care for the wounded and the homeless. This was done very neatly; the army was in and out, no permament presence of any kind; Slayton and the Two left on the first flight. There were a few rude remarks in the local press, but these will be forgotten in time. N—— is back to normal. I had one small satisfaction, which I shared with my wife the night we put together the rescue plan. Since the operation was an agency matter from the beginning, I insisted that we be given overall control; that is, one of our people in the field supervising the army units under orders from me. This is a departure from the normal procedure, and it took me twelve hours to fight it out with the Pentagon; but we prevailed, and I directed the operation from my desk in Washington. I was in personal charge, so it fell to me to choose a code name. I chose the name Sylvia.

Burns

Anonymous then, Burns joined the State Department in May of 1959, the week John Foster Dulles died. He carried with him a letter of introduction from his history tutor at Columbia, but was never able to use it because the dying secretary was refused visitors. Burns tucked the letter away, sad because he admired the old man's Bourbon audacity (nothing learned, nothing forgotten) and wanted to meet him; he disapproved of the *weltanschauung* but liked the *geist*. He'd arrived in Washington with two suitcases and a half-dozen cartons of books, all of it stuffed into the rear seat of a red Volkswagen. An officer of the Foreign Service of the United States of America. Diplomatic immunity. A black passport. He and a friend from Columbia rented a small furnished house in Foggy Bottom, within easy walking distance of the department, and the summer passed pleasantly, without incident.

Burns was eager, trained in economics and an accomplished linguist as well: excellent German, French, and Italian, passable Russian. Intelligent, watchful, Burns had a thoughtful nature, and his career proceeded logically and without sensation. The first year, he was assigned to the European section as a cable clerk. Burns found the State Department agreeable, he liked its stillness and atmosphere of deliberation, quiet days broken only by the odd hasty moments when the entire section would turn to, drafting instructions for an ambassador or a memorandum for the secretary. The department was a forest of hat racks, scholarly in its way; Burns was reminded of low-keyed university seminars. That first year, he spent much of his time with the head of the German desk, listening to droll stories of Berlin in the 1930s; the head of the German desk had known Dorothy Thompson and Christopher Isherwood and was a nimble raconteur.

The second year he was posted to Turkey, stamping passports, and the next three years were spent in Bonn, in the office of the economic counselor. These were rewarding and exciting years; Burns felt he was doing useful work and was wise enough to take frequent holidays throughout Europe. He saw all of Germany and the Low Countries and most of Switzerland and France, and passed one Christmas in Rome with friends. In somnolent Bad Godesberg he lived in a small suite in the Yankee ghetto, the large bleak block of flats near the embassy that the American government had built as a communal residence. No living off the land! The staff hated its isolation. Burns did not mind; he could walk to the Rhine, and he had a girl friend who lived on the Nibelungenstrasse. The ghetto was amusing in its way, Mother America caring for her children, the government surrounding you even as you slept; but the building was truly inelegant. The part of the job that he hated was the necessary contact with traveling American businessmen, many of whom thought that the State Department was a division of the U.S. Chamber of Commerce.

Burns cultivated objectivity: he was no good at all out front.

His record was excellent and studded with commendations. He was discreet, reliable, and hardworking. By the time he left Bonn, Burns knew most of the important older German labor leaders and all of the unimportant younger ones. Burns was building for the future, for the day ten years hence when he'd return. He got on well with the younger Germans, finding to his surprise that he shared their taste for the livid and the grotesque: gargantuan meals, carnival sideshows, Grosz and Brecht, and the underground university theater. Burns often filled in for the cultural attaché at benefits and openings, and at embassy receptions for visiting American artists and writers. Through his contacts in the German labor movement and his skillful analysis of the direction of the German economy, he was brought into frequent contact with the deputy chief of mission, a diplomat of long and varied experience. The DCM encouraged his career and coached him in the ways of the department. Burns particularly remembered one bit of advice, given late one night over schnapps:

"The department values loyalty, intelligence, and calm — in that order. The Foreign Service is something apart from the run-of-the-mill American bureaucracy. Remember that. We are not action people, we are analysts. Leave the action to the pickle factory and the Pentagon, they are the ones with the resources (and the ones who'll evade the blame). Stay close to the bureaucracy," Burns was told. "It is an elite, and the better for it. Not as elite, mind you, as it was. But elite nonetheless. Study diplomatic technique. Read history. Always be cautious, always be firm . . ."

"Firmly cautious or cautiously firm?" Burns inquired with a flicker of a smile.

"Very," said the DCM.

Burns was surprised and disappointed in the fall of 1965 when he was ordered back to Washington and informed he was being loaned to CIA. He was told only that the agency had a major project under way which required the participation of many of their economists. It left them short-handed, and meanwhile the State Department had been directed by Congress to cut its own budget. The loan would not be for long, perhaps no more than one year. Burns should think of it as a net plus, if not a clear advantage; he could have been transferred to AID. He'd been requested by name, and the transfer had the blessing of the department.

The first day at Langley he was shown his office, and it was not in the German section, as he'd been told.

"Here you are," the chief of section said. "Everything you'll need. Paper, pencils, slide rule, computer room down the hall. Filing cabinets there. Toilet down the hall and to your right. Staff meeting every day at nine, and sometimes again at six."

"I thought it'd be the German —"

"This is not the German."

"Yes, but I was told the arrangement."

"That is on another floor. That is on the third floor, quite different and apart from this. That is another section, something distinctly separate from what we do here."

"I know, but ..."

"You can ask them about it. You'll get an answer. Perhaps there was a snafu. There sometimes is. Are. Snafus."

"Son of a bitch," Burns said.

"You were in Bonn?"

"Three years."

"Well, they probably thought that a change of scene . . ."

"But I am an FSO."

"You'll come to like it here," the chief of section said.

The first year at Langley was disagreeable in all but one respect. Burns watched the bureaucratic gavotte as it was danced by experts and learned lessons he never forgot. They were lessons in bureaucratic technique, and the uses of firmness and caution. At first, Burns told himself that these were lessons he wished he did not know, but he found out that once known they were impossible to ignore or forget; in the beginning, he thought it was like learning something damaging or unpleasant about a friend. The friendship changes, usually for the worse — and yes, yes, he knew it was naïve and unrealistic but it was the way he felt nevertheless. He found himself admiring the small ways a man moved ahead, the ways in which a man identified the winners and then placed his bets. There was no question of political or ideological conflict — the agency was too sophisticated for that; it was mainly a matter of technology and the skill with which a bureaucrat managed to force his ideas, and thereby gain a purchase on the future. In CIA Burns was able to learn with a clear and objective mind, because he was a man on loan; in time he would be returned to the State Department, where he belonged.

Burns had no ax to grind, but the department dawdled amid procedural inertia and the budgetary restraints imposed by Congress. Burns remained at Langley although he yearned for the security and familiarity of the Foreign Service, the satisfaction of fashioning American foreign policy; he felt himself an artist among artisans, made few close friends, and denounced (privately) the rules and regulations, which seemed to him frivolous when they were not corrupting. The spooks ran as a pack and considered him an outsider. But the job had its moments. Paper. He tried to explain it, his life inside the bureaucracy. Burns translated French documents relating to the economy of a small African nation, a small, *pivotal* African nation, in the vernacular of the Board of National Estimates. Every day the documents arrived in pouch, and Burns would translate them and summarize the contents. Some of them were official, some not; some of them were agents' reports. The précis went to the chief of section, who would include it in the running commentary on the economy and politics of the country.

"Think of yourself as Charles Dickens," the chief of section told Burns. "Writing a novel, a new installment every month. Odd turnings of plot. But a bold metaphor. Except that this novel goes on forever and forever, of course."

"A sort of *Pickwick Papers* in triplicate," Burns said.

"You've got it exactly," the chief replied.

The government of the small, pivotal African nation was fledgling and incompetent, and one week, the reports said, owned by the Russians, the next by the Chinese. Conscientious Burns received State Department cables as well (there were channels), and these he eagerly awaited, particularly the commentary of the chief political officer, a sardonic and witty diplomat who doubted everything, including agents' reports: "Buy the government? You can't even rent it for an afternoon." For the first two years the work was interesting, and even valid in a perverse way. The prime minister had committed "significant errors" in the management of his country's finances, and it was beguiling — often amusing — to try to put the pieces of fact together to make a comprehensible whole. Burns threw himself into it, juggling trade figures, cash flow, tax revenues, production, employment, resource management, inflation, and all the other classical indices of economic fortune. One afternoon he created an entirely fictitious Gross National Product, which he dropped in his out box on a lark. It turned up later in the National Estimate, and that worried Burns. At the time, the country was on the verge of collapse, indeed the statistics indicated the country had collapsed. According to the numbers, the bottom line as Burns called it, the country was bankrupt and not functioning — except that it continued as before, the vitality and innocence of the people defying all known economic laws, or anyway those laws that were promulgated by American economists. Burns conceived the novel idea that his statistics had nothing whatever to do with the situation. Novel to Burns, not novel to his section chief.

"You're learning," the chief said.

"Remember the GNP figure?" Burns was in the mood for a confession.

"Four hundred eighty-two point something-something million? Sure."

"It was all cock," Burns said. "Doesn't exist."

"Strange," the chief mused. "It seemed to fit in so well."

"Some of the figures were real. But I made most of them up. The GNP is meaningless."

"Yes," the chief said sadly.

"I'll play around with it again, if you'd like me to. Perhaps a new figure . . ."

"Please do."

"I suppose I shouldn't have said anything."

"It doesn't matter," the chief said. "So long as I know."

"Well, I'm sorry if it's embarrassing in any way."

The chief looked at him, surprised. "Why should I be embarrassed?"

Burns was nearing the end of two years in National Estimates, and most of his friends were overseas, some of them in Southeast Asia, where the wars were being fought, and their infrequent letters home made him long for the symmetry and rhythm of the State Department, anything real. He became nostalgic, recalling the details of his flat in the ghetto and the look of the Rhine at dawn, during his salad days in Bonn. He remembered the long talks with the DCM, and his satisfaction at filing skillful reports. Now he'd been passed by. One man he had known briefly in the embassy at Bonn had actually been a member of the working party negotiating the test ban treaty with the Soviet Union. His former roommate was ADC to the ambassador in Saigon, and that man was Burns's own age and grade. Other friends were in Europe or the Middle East, living well in Amsterdam or Beirut. Meanwhile, Burns reflected bitterly, he pushed paper at CIA and watched experts maneuver the bureaucracy. His polite requests for return to the State Department elicited polite replies, mere acknowledgments, no more.

In the evenings in Washington, home alone with his drinks and his dog, Burns would undertake National Estimates of his own life. A personal GNP, entirely factual and aboveboard. Big, bearish, awkward Burns, b. 1937 N.Y.C., father an M.D., mother a psychologist, "professional people." Medical talk at the breakfast table, mind-numbing Saturday afternoons at Yankee Stadium: good father, obedient son. But his childhood and adolescence were mostly blank, seventeen blank years until he entered Columbia University, became fascinated with economics and history, graduated with honors, and joined the Foreign Service. This became the central objective of his life, membership in the Diplomatic Corps and an understanding of the interplay ("the confusion") of politics and economics. The stress was on manipulation and management — of national interests, of alliances, of various political and economic crises, all of it huddled together under Reason and the Rule of Law. It was no place for an eccentric. Burns admired professional diplomats — men who were cool, collected, in control, rising to a geopolitical *crisis* (he liked the word — his doctor father first defined it for him as the point in the course of a disease when the patient either recovers or dies). He saw himself as one of a dozen men in a small room, an anteroom in a foreign chancellery (Belgrade? Helsinki?), conducting secret negotiations, ADC to a giant, Bohlen or Kennan, taking on the Russians, and by sheer force of logic and remorseless dialectic, arguing them back, turning their own deceptions against them. Forcing an agreement, and then a laconic cable to the department: *Negotiations concluded* ...

But that was a joke now. What he had to show for eight years in the Diplomatic Service were a few commendations, and some flimsies of cables he'd sent. He had a Q Security Clearance; now he could read intercepts from anywhere, from Havana or Hanoi or Pyongyang. And he had a filing cabinet full of economic analysis of a wretched country which had, if the analysis were correct, collapsed. He had all those things plus a flat stomach, owing in part to his noontime squash games with an overweight colonel who was, similarly, on loan to CIA. He did not know the colonel's job, and did not want to know.

To an empty room, at midnight on a Monday night: "Celebrated Diplomat. Superspy Burns, the hired gun. The cloak-and-dagger man from National Estimates. A fast man with a document, that Burns. Hard. Resourceful. Adroit."

Burns was a man of routine, at home as at his office. There were no crises in his section of the agency, so he arrived home in Foggy Bottom punctually at seven each evening. He'd feed the dog and select a recording with great care; a different recording each night. He prepared a shaker of cocktails, and at nine would put a steak on the grill and frozen potatoes in the oven. He stood at the counter in the kitchen, drinking his drink and slowly breaking lettuce into a salad bowl. As the steak cooked, he selected his wine. The wine selected, Burns moved to his bookcase for the evening's read. Something British, he thought, and ran his thumb along the spines of his books. Disraeli. Cromwell. Melbourne. Yes, Melbourne — William Lamb, alone and distracted at the end of his life, the affections of Victoria detached from him and fastened on another. Melbourne, the quintessence of controlled inaction. He prowled among the books, glass in hand, then paused. He had not read his latest issue of *Revue de Défense Nationale*, the authoritative guide to the thinking of the French general staff. It was there now, arrived in the morning mail, on the coffee table, unopened, waiting. He glanced through the table of contents. Arms control. The Indian subcontinent. Ah. General J. Nemo would bear careful evaluation: "Etude sur la guerre de Vendée (II)."

Burns smelled the steak and the potatoes and returned to the kitchen. He uncorked the wine and set it gently on the table. He'd set his place that morning, the knife, fork, and spoon on one side of the plate, the wooden salt and pepper shakers to his left, the white napkin folded just so, a fresh candle in the silver holder. Then Burns sat down with the steak and the potatoes, the salad and the wine, and began to read "Etude sur la guerre de Vendée (II)." Inside his mind, General J. Nemo competed with the memory of a candlelit dinner in Munich four years ago. The dinner was followed by visits to half a dozen nightclubs, ending at dawn. Burns finished in thirty minutes, then slowly washed and wiped the dishes and the silverware. He spoke to the dog and returned to the living room, where the backgammon board was waiting.

He carefully prepared his pipe with the tobacco purchased that evening and bent over the board, playing both sides, but mentally betting on white. He smoked three pipes, then lay back on the couch, thinking.

"Nemo appears to have got hold of something interesting in the new *Revue*. Pertinent to our own situation, it seems to me."

"I haven't seen . . . that number."

"I recommend Nemo and Mourin."

"Ah, Mourin. The historian."

"Some new insights into the Sovs on the subcontinent."

"How much time do you spend on that stuff?"

"Well, not much; I read it, is about all."

"Blast, I wish I could find the time."

"Important stuff."

"Burns, you're bullshitting me."

Every Friday night Burns and five others forgathered at one house or another to play poker or backgammon. Except for Burns on loan, all of them were State Department people. By civil servant standards, the stakes were high: at backgammon, a dollar a point; at poker, a ten-dollar limit. Burns, bearish over the backgammon board, was the big winner. He played a loose, conservative game — with occasional light and daring moments, when he felt the dice were right or when he found himself in untenable positions. He lived on the backgammon board, absorbing himself in the moves, studying probabilities, odds this way and that. Straitlaced men tended to be erratic at games, and Burns watched for the break, the wrong move when the dice were cold or the odds close, but not close enough.

More interesting than chess, because the dice were thirty percent of it — all other things being equal, which they never were. The edge was in the double; he paid attention to the utility of the double. The psychological double or the administrative double or the deceptive double.

It was rather like diplomacy in that way, and as interesting, because Burns had learned the fanciful nature of world affairs. A carapace of madness, concealing the tortoise beneath; the revisionists saw it the other way around, but the revisionists were wrong. He inspected the men around the tables, all of them young like himself and ambitious in diplomacy; they had outflanked him, their careers were secure. The dice rattled, the counters flashed: doubled here, redoubled there. Acceptance. Refusal. Failure of entry. He played backgammon now as a substitute for diplomacy. Dulles was dead, had died the year he came to Washington. The letter of introduction hadn't been worth a damn.

2

THEY knew *what* had happened, that was clear enough. They also knew, within limits, *how* it happened. They were less certain about the *who* and the *why*. But the government of the pivotal African nation had fallen, and the capital was now in the hands of insurgents. These were insurgents from the army and from the economics ministry, something of a queer alliance: the army officers were presumed to be reactionaries and the economists Communists. At ten in the morning they met in urgent session, representatives from the agency, the Pentagon, the State Department, and the White House. They met downtown in the Executive Office Building, entering underground. Burns was in on it, as the agency man closest to the economics ministry. They had tried to hash it out beforehand.

"Names, Burns, do you have names? You can bet your booties that the Pentagon will have names. Christ, they'll have a file on every colonel in that ragtag army. Half of them probably attended Leavenworth."

"I'll ransack the files."

"You do that, Burns. Do that right away."

But in Burns's section they had not concentrated on names. They had assembled numbers, numbers of bewildering variety and degree. They knew the names of the economics minister and his deputy, and the chief adviser to the prime minister. But these were not men who would participate in a revolt. These were men who were in the pay of others, or were said to be. So Burns went to the files and spent a feverish hour rummaging through them. The warning — the opportunity! — rang in his ears.

"Burns, we want control of this operation. If there *is* an operation. We've got men on the ground, we've got very good op-con. American interests are involved, and don't forget that. This is what the deputy director wants, and that is what we will have. But you've got to find the names. And give identity to the names . . ."

The meeting began slowly. Burns noted with satisfaction that there were two dozen men in the room, four or five from each agency. It meant there would have to be a second meeting. The Pentagon man, an army general, spoke first, and it was an astonishing stroke of luck because he was inarticulate and ill at ease with the gallicized African names. The deputy director scored a point straight-away.

"Our intelligence indicates that the leader is a major," the Pentagon man said. "Name's Hubert . . . Fooshing?"

"Ah yes," the DD said. "Ooo-bear. Foo-saw."

"You know him?" the Pentagon man inquired politely.

"Burns knows him," the DD said. "But we'll get to that later."

Rattled, the army general continued with his briefing. It was a disorganized briefing, but the names had been there. There were about two dozen names in all, mostly mispronounced. All the facts were there — ominous, compelling — but it required an effort of will to organize them. Burns saw the DD smile and make notes on the back of an envelope.

The representative of the State Department followed, and Burns sat back in his chair and listened. It was a *tour d'horizon*, the politics and economics of the country briefly, brilliantly, sketched. The geography and demographics of the country, its relations with its neighbors, its natural resources, its investments. There was a side excursion into cultural anthropology, a long reach back into prehistory for the national metaphors. Burns was dazzled; the State Department man had them in the palm of his hand. Finally, almost casually, he brought them up to the present moment, and the question of the American interest. This was done lucidly and skillfully, a history of diplomatic relations between the world's most powerful nation and one of the world's weakest. The diplomat stood at the head of the table, his hands in his pockets, speaking without notes.

A low, musical voice: "The truth of the matter is this, gentlemen. The United States has no interest in this country. Sad, but true. Lamentable if the country falls to the Communists — Russians, Chinese, Cuban, whomever . . ." Burns noted the correct "whomever" and nodded in appreciation. "But in any serious analysis, not important. Too much risk against no gain. Gentlemen, let us leave them be. And remember the Armenian proverb: *A thousand men cannot undress a naked man.*"

He'd taken it all, ears and tail, hooves and bull.

The DD said nothing for a moment; Burns watched his jaw work. In the general conversation that followed the State Department presentation, he heard the DD mutter, "Oh fuck," but no one else heard. Now he was in a jam: not only had he to outmatch the diplomat's logic, but his elegance of speech as well. Burns watched the DD rise, and pause for dramatic effect.

"I hope none of us falls into the trap of disregarding the fate of a sovereign nation simply because it is small," the DD said. "Or black. Or without resources. Or generally friendless in a hostile world. Or in the fist of revolution" — not bad, Burns thought — "its national identity not yet fully forged from the tangled threads of its own tribal history and the odious legacy of colonial exploitation. A nation without a center of gravity. A nation which looks to the United States of America for leadership . . ."

"Last month they burned down the embassy," the State Department man murmured, just loud enough to be heard.

"*They* didn't, the *Communists* did. And that's the difference. Easy for us here in the capital of the United States to shrug off this *minor*" — the word was spoken harshly —

"country's agony, these infaust events . . ." *Infaust*, Burns thought: the DD was pulling every lever he possessed. There weren't a dozen people in Washington who knew what the word meant — except of course the diplomat, who nodded, slight smile.

Burns was anxious, the DD made a good case. He was pulling the levers available to him. The diplomat had not been specific, he'd given them a brilliant *tour d'horizon*, nothing more. Presently the DD lapsed into fact, so much American investment, the strategic value of the Nbororo river, the threat to peaceful neighbors.

"I think we ought to very carefully consider putting a team in on the ground. Civilians, no more than forty or fifty. But before we come to that, I would like Burns to say a word about the sort of men who run the economy of . . . this 'naked' country."

Well played, Burns thought. He rose, a tightness in his throat. The DD had them now; they could not ignore the facts. Facts were the DD's strong suit, and now he was calling on Burns to back him up. The DD looked at him, encouraging a strong response. Burns stared across the table at the diplomat, hands loosely clasped on the table. The diplomat's expression was benign; he'd made his case. That was the trouble with the State Department. They didn't *fight;* they were gentlemen. They didn't read each other's mail. Well, they deserved what they got, Burns thought. If they did not control events, events would control them. Laissez-faire had its limits. For Castlereagh, Chamberlain. Burns cleared his throat.

"There is no question they will expropriate American properties," Burns said. Then he named the economists, two who had received instruction at Lumumba University, Moscow; a third from Havana; two or three others who'd cruised through the L.S.E. "One of these" — he mentioned a name and an age — "has unusually strong ties with the ... black movement ... in the United States. So there is a domestic political spin to all this ..."

The agency, at that meeting and at later meetings, carried the day. Forty men were dispatched up the Nbororo river in rafts. They landed and reported the town quiet. There was no shooting, nor any signs of upheaval. The communications worked splendidly. In time, most of them returned. There was a different government, but no expropriations.

They were good about it. They wanted him to stay, to "pack it in" for keeps at the State Department and become permanently attached to the agency. They liked him. Burns did intelligent, careful work. Sometimes, when the problem truly interested him, he was brilliant. They indicated to him, but delicately, that his habits were somewhat bizarre — but fully within the ...

"Ah, parameters."

"Of what?"

"Behavior, acceptable."

"Oh, yes."

"Look, Burns. If you will do no more than trouble yourself to get an M.A., preferably in your field, economics, the future here is very bright, very very bright. Limitless, really."

"Forget economics, how about this, something stronger? An M.A. in the diplomatic history of Europe."

"Not as good, but acceptable."

"The . . . Eastern religions?"

The personnel man smiled. There were already more ersatz Buddhists than the agency could comfortably tolerate. SEA Section smelled like an incense factory, gnomic sayings sprouted like tulips. No, definitely not "the Eastern religions."

"Too bad," Burns said.

"Look, if you're tired of Africa, we can . . ."

"I am tired of Africa, Africa is tired of me," Burns said.

"All right, we understand that. Like pinning Jell-O to the wall, no?"

Burns smiled.

"So let us turn elsewhere."

"The field," Burns said, and the personnel man shook his head. No, not possible. Burns was an inside man, an analyst from the inside; anyone could see that. Outside men were something else altogether. Burns wasn't one of those, probably wouldn't ever be.

The personnel man was encouraging. He tempted Burns. "Look. One immediate jump in grade. That's a couple of thou a year more for you. What will it be? Seventeen, seventeen-five. You have another income. You can move to Georgetown. Or Chevy Chase, and really go with the high rollers."

Burns was expressionless, though surprised. But of course they would know about the gambling.

". . . A couple of thou more a year."

Burns smiled bleakly; he had no need of money.

"And a change of venue." The personnel man mentioned two countries, one in Asia and the other in Latin America.

The Latin American country was an interesting proposition, no doubt about it. Its economy had even less to recommend it than the African. But other aspects were more favorable. It was clearly a nation in crisis.

"Not exactly the Soviet Union, is it?"

The personnel man smiled and shrugged.

"Or Germany."

"You know the ropes here now. You know us, we know you. We all get along together. We don't have to finish sentences, do we? Saves us a lot of bother both ways, no?"

"I suppose it does."

"There's another compensation. If you take the LatAm job, you can go down there for six weeks, see the place yourself. Eyeball it firsthand. We'll set you up. We're very liberal about that sort of thing, as you know. On your way down you can stop off at Puerto Rico, Freeport . . ."

"For the casinos?"

The personnel man smiled.

"Who do you think I am, Nick the Greek?"

". . . Break up the return trip in Jamaica, Tobago."

"Six weeks, you say."

"More or less."

Burns mused: "It takes time to really get into these countries. They're complicated. The people, the statistics. It takes time to know what makes them tick . . ."

"This place is no Girard-Perregaux, Burns."

"And when I get back?"

The personnel man explained the job again, and its title. The location of the office, and the men immediately above and below him. His superior would be a man sixty-one years old, near retirement. Burns would be in line. From there would come a shot at the secretariat itself, the board. If everything broke right, Burns would be on the front line, on the inside, at forty-five, forty-six years old.

"I've always thought about the field."

The personnel man said nothing and looked at the clock on the wall.

"Give me a week to decide?"

"Of course."

"I want to check in with some friends at State. Get another opinion. It's a radical move."

"State's agreeable," the personnel man said quickly.

"Oh?"

"Quite agreeable."

Burns shook his head. His old friend the DCM in Bonn was correct. Once he'd left the department, there was no returning. He'd left their files, become a memory attached to another agency. Others now competed for attention. It always happened in government; once you broke your career chain it was curtains, and you ceased to exist. You were elsewhere, no longer in their control. Burns supposed that the State Department suspected that he'd picked up bad habits at Langley; they assumed no one ever *quit* the place, as indeed no one ever did. The procedures were different, and these would become habits that would divide his loyalties. That was the other thing they thought about, the loyalty of the man to his agency. That was critical, particularly if you were truly of the bureaucracy and on your way up, not an inner and outer, but a career professional man. If your loyalty were divided, there was no end of potential disagreement and therefore of conflict and strife. You were not a man whom they could count on in a crisis.

"I'll tell you in a week," Burns said.

"I don't understand this one thing," the personnel man said. "What exactly is your reluctance? You've a clear shot here."

"I always wanted to be a diplomat."

"Well, there's a lot of action here. More than the other place. You're doing essentially the same thing, analysis. It's just going into a different pipeline. And of course —"

"You know, the Congress of Vienna."

"— you're anonymous."

"That's the only thing that appeals to me," Burns said.

Prime Evening Time

H E told his wife that the most important fact of his war duty was that he'd survived it. He made the statement once in Hawaii, when they were reunited, again in San Francisco, when they deplaned, and several times in the car, driving from the West Coast to the East. On the remainder he was silent. She hated the war, although she was very proud of him, and did not insist on details. The details would only depress and frighten her and she told him that she would rather not know them.

He was an infantry captain, and in the course of three years in the war zone had won a Bronze Star, three Silver Stars, and, finally, the Medal of Honor. He looked at the last with a certain ambiguity, because he'd won it while leading a company of men into an ambush. Possessing natural skills, he'd performed creditably well and did not know until a week after the fire fight that his CO had put him in for the Congressional, the highest decoration an American soldier could receive. He'd gotten it a year later, somewhat to his embarrassment. The captain did not grieve, however, because his Bronze Star should have been a Medal of Honor; in that action, he'd managed to save lives, perhaps as many as twenty or thirty lives, and his company had all but destroyed an enemy battalion.

In Washington they wanted him visible, so they made

him a staff assistant to the chairman of the joint chiefs of staff. After his tours in the war zone, he accepted the assignment with pleasure, because he'd have an opportunity to meet the men who actually made policy. Soon to make major, the captain assumed that his future with the army was secure; he'd done three tours in the war, and that was enough.

The captain kept his wife separate from his work. For all she knew about him he might have been an insurance salesman or a dentist, except of course for the uniform that he wore, and the telephone calls at odd hours. Their life centered around casual things, the house in the suburbs, their army friends, the occasional holidays south. The captain did not carry work home with him, and in fact it was mostly military trivia, nickels and dimes. The captain shuffled papers from one box to another and attended daily meetings, spear-carrying for senior officers. He wrote reports and conducted briefings for distinguished visitors, including members of Congress. The captain was "known," in an imprecise way; from his bearing and his correct manner, visitors rightly assumed him to be one of the army's bright young men. From time to time he was trotted out on display by the army public relations office, so he was not surprised one morning to receive a telephone call from the chief of information, an elderly and argumentative colonel whom he'd known in the war.

"Do you know Charles O'Brien?"

"I don't know him," the captain said. "But I listen to him."

"Well, his network is doing a special on war veterans. War heros, according to O'Brien. He tells me it's going to

be a sympathetic show — that's the word he used, 'sympathetic' — on combat troops. Very favorable to the army.
No cheap shots. Now he's particularly interested —"

"Negative," the captain said. "Respectfully, sir, negative."

"Wait a minute. O'Brien is not a prick. I've known him
on and off for years. I knew him in the real war. He's the
anchor man and this thing is going to run in prime evening
time." The colonel's voice dropped. "He showed me a list
of our people that they want to interview. It's going to be
all army, mostly infantry. No sailors, no fly-boys. All
army, do you understand? Now this list. It's a hell of a
good list, and your name is at the top of it. Because you're
such a hell of a war hero."

The captain sighed.

"O'Brien specifically wants you, hotshot. And he did not
come to me with the request. He went straight to the old
man, and the old man said that if he wanted you he could
have you. Old man's orders."

The captain thought a minute, knowing now that argument was useless. "I knew some of them overseas, and I
didn't like them except for one or two."

The colonel snorted with contempt. "As far as I'm concerned, they're war criminals. They're the enemy, and a
concentration camp is too good for them, but O'Brien's
something else." The colonel's temper flared and subsided.
"O'Brien's all right. He's a different echelon altogether."

"Sure. You bet."

"Anyway, I'm sure you can work it out. I'm sure you
can come to terms with it in your own mind. Because it's
orders."

"Thanks, Colonel."

"Anytime, Captain. I'll tell the old man that you're delighted and honored to participate. That you're a good soldier. That you want to do your part for the army's image."

"Yes, sir."

"In front of about thirty million people, give or take a few. That's the audience in prime evening time."

"When will they be around? When does it start?" The captain's voice was hoarse and confused. He'd been obliged to deal with correspondents when he won the Medal of Honor, and a couple of them had managed to slice him up. The war lover, an animal. One of them made him sound like Goebbels.

"Next week, week after. They want to get this thing 'in the can,' as they say, before the current offensive is ended." The colonel paused and chuckled softly. "You see, it has news value. They want to run it while there's still a lot of action overseas. While the casualty figures are still high."

"Christ," the captain said.

That night, having a drink with his wife, the captain worried the problem. He told his wife that the television people never got anything straight, and it was very difficult talking about what they wanted him to talk about. It was not something that was easily articulated, you either understood it or you didn't and there wasn't any satisfactory explanation. The other thing was that he was back in Washington now and wanted to forget about the war. He was not ashamed of it or bored with it, but it was another part of his life and he wanted to get on to other things. He was proud of what he had done, and very proud of the Medal of Honor. But it was an emotion he preferred to keep to himself. His wife, not understanding the motivation, thought that he was being selfish.

"If it'll help the army, why not?"

"I suppose," he said glumly.

"It can't do any harm."

"Yes it can," he said sharply. She looked at him, startled. "It's hard to explain."

The truth was that he believed they were *his* medals, honorably earned. They were *his* experiences and when it came to that, *his* survival. The medals were part of his own history, they were evidence of things seen with his own eyes. Burned in his own memory. All these things were personal, and the captain thought that he was entitled to keep them to himself.

So his wife was partly correct after all.

They recorded two preliminary interviews and then arranged a shooting schedule. The interviews had gone so well (or so they told him) that O'Brien decided to build the entire show around the captain. Others would be interviewed, but the captain would be the centerpiece. They'd sent two reporters to conduct the preliminaries, one to ask questions and the other to operate the tape recorder. They taped the entire interview but the reporter took notes anyway. Then they fixed the first day's shooting, and when the captain learned of its location he immediately telephoned the chief of information.

"Do you know where they're doing it, Colonel? Do you know? Did they tell you?"

"They told me," the colonel said.

"Arlington," the captain said, his voice incredulous and furious at the same time.

"O'Brien's idea." The colonel was beyond surprise.

"But *Christ!*"

"Well, that's the way they want it. And they've got the old man's blessing."

"Perched on a tombstone, I suppose."

"No, actually not. We've got a copy of the shooting script. Minus your lines, of course. Just a general outline. They're going to shoot you standing, with the gravestones behind you in a long line. I was worried about it, too, but the way they're doing it will be kind of I'd guess you'd say heroic. Not depressing, but heroic."

"Oh, I see. Heroic."

"Well, dramatic."

"Dramatic-heroic."

The colonel laughed and said nothing.

"Colonel . . ."

"That's showbiz, baby."

"But they can screw me up."

"No, they think you're a natural. Good-looking, modest. Intelligent, a warm and positive personality. Reserved, a good voice. A model soldier. They're going to tout you as the chief of staff of the future."

"How will that set upstairs?" the captain asked after a moment.

"Don't worry, the old man thinks it's outstanding. He's taking a personal interest. He and O'Brien are on the phone every other day. The old man himself is going to do a short interview at the end of the show."

"So he's not angry in any way."

The colonel laughed. "I never knew you to have problems with generals."

"It's the first time I've been involved . . . in this way."

"Yes. There's one other thing. I've arranged a briefing for you this afternoon on one or two suggested topics. Now, they're going to get into the conditions over there, and your response to that will be positive. If they ask about equipment, your response to that will be *very* positive. And it would be well for you to suggest that there's been a lot of bloodshed. You know, so the dinks can be free. Got that?" The colonel coughed. "Other than that, you're on your own."

"One of your guys will be there, I hope. To monitor."

"Unh-unh," the colonel said. "That was one of the arrangements with O'Brien. No PIOs at all, not even me. Just you and the cameras and the microphones and the reporters."

"In the graveyard at Arlington."

"You'll figure a way. Bye-bye, General."

"Yes, sir," the captain said.

They decided to film at dusk, three successive days since the light was right ("moody") for only about an hour and a half. The first day, they staged a military funeral that would be barely visible, blurred, through the camera's lens. That would be in the background, with the gravestones in the middle distance, and the captain up front. They told him that they intended to edit the sound track so that there would be no questions, only answers. Anyone looking at the film would assume that the captain was talking spontaneously, not responding to a reporter's interrogation.

Charles O'Brien hoped for an impression of stark and melancholy drama. A Stephen Crane short story, he told his reporters and cameramen; spare, deeply sympathetic, *and no irony*.

The captain arrived the first afternoon wearing his suntans, with only two ribbons: the combat infantryman's badge and the paratrooper insignia. He'd brought along the others in an attaché case, in the event they wanted him to wear them. The assistant producer called O'Brien in New York to ask him about it, and O'Brien said that the captain could wear what he wanted. O'Brien said he liked the idea of a minimum of ribbons. It gave the impression of soldierliness: lean, austere, modest, manly.

They began to film in the late afternoon, the captain standing next to a Civil War gravestone. The main camera was only ten feet from him, it obstructed his view of the cemetery. A second camera was located on a bluff a quarter of a mile away. This camera would give them a long shot from time to time, the captain and his suite of technicians almost invisible among the gravestones; then the long lens would pull him into focus very slowly, the captain's tall figure becoming gradually more prominent, the distance between the lens and the man foreshortened. The audience would feel isolation and loneliness. The camera's lens was a quarter of a mile away but the man's voice was up close, a disorienting conjunction of distance and intimacy; O'Brien thought the combination would be stunning, if the captain spoke the right lines. The reporter stood behind the close camera and one of the enormous lights, feeding questions.

"How did you come to join the army, Captain?"

"Do you intend to make it your permanent career?"

"Can you describe the military life?"

"How many medals do you have, Captain?"

"Well, sir, there are the Mickey Mouse medals that everyone gets. Good-conduct ribbons, campaign medals, this medal and that. The important ones that I have are the three Silver Stars, the Bronze, and of course the Medal of Honor."

"How did you get the Medal of Honor?"

"Sir?"

"The Medal of Honor. What did you do to win it?"

"Well, sir."

The reporter motioned to the cameraman to cut and walked over to the soldier. "Captain, this is kind of embarrassing. But I think it'd be better if you didn't say 'sir.' What we're after here is an even flow, just a guy standing on a hill talking about the war and the way people fight . . . the wars. What separates the good soldiers from the bad. What it takes, or doesn't take, to win a Silver Star. Why one man is good at it and another not. Just what makes a soldier, in other words. Just a nice easy flow, natural, and don't become disconcerted if the camera moves away. Most of this will be a voice-over, your voice heard while the scene the viewers are watching is the long row of gravestones or the funeral over there. We're thinking of splicing in some battle footage, all of it, or some of it, in slow motion . . ." The captain tried to concentrate on the words that came so smoothly. The reporter had a deep voice and enunciated carefully. "We've got a bit of film of you in the war zone, and we'll splice that in too. You know, a little *cinéma vérité*. Very effective. But your words are going to carry the scene, it's what you're *saying* that will make the impact. So the objective is for you to be as relaxed and natural as you can. Now just go ahead, about the Medal of Honor."

"Well, it isn't the easiest . . ."

"I understand." The reporter was sympathetic, his voice soothing. "But we can edit, cut, and fit. Don't worry, it's fine so far. You ready?"

"Now?"

"When the red light's on. Now."

"Medal of Honor's the highest award a man can win in the military service . . ."

". . . but this is very, very difficult to put into words. I guess you begin with an enjoyment of the physical life, comradeship with other men, that sort of thing. I guess it's partly a test, you're testing yourself against yourself and against others. That's one part of it, you want to excel, and of course there's no tougher place than a battlefield. It's no football field. You make a mistake and it's not only your own life, but if you're an officer, a leader, it's the lives of other men. The responsibility is enormous. I don't know of anything, any other field of endeavor, where it's any greater . . ."

"Excellent, Captain. Really first-rate. Talk a bit more about the responsibility. Were you ever in a situation where a decision of yours cost lives?"

"Certainly. Any decision you make in battle costs lives, in one way or another."

"Talk now about the most important decision you ever made. How you came to make it, and so forth."

"Well, that's interesting. That's a good question. It was in my third tour . . ."

The captain found that after a while he forgot about the television cameras and the reporter. By turning his face slightly to the left he presented a profile and avoided the light. As he talked he looked over the Civil War gravestones and the big oak trees beyond. He developed a technique of pausing, just before he ran out of words. He'd pause for five or six seconds, then resume his monologue. He found that it had a strange, hypnotic effect on him, as if he were reading from an invisible script; he never skipped a beat. After the first session, one of the cameramen told him it was the best thing he'd ever filmed, and by "best" the cameraman meant "genuine."

The captain discovered that it was possible to slide over details that halted the flow of language. These were unimportant details. In retelling one anecdote he'd misplaced the scene of the action. In another, he'd slightly underestimated the number of dead. In a third he mispronounced a man's name. None of these slight errors had an effect on the overall theme.

"It's strange," he told his wife after the second day's filming. "But I sort of like it, it's interesting to do."

"Why not? You like what you're good at."

"Well, I was opposed to the whole idea. Those press bastards. But it's important that the public understand these things, things about the war. They're important. There is a war on after all, and the public ought to understand what it means to actually fight it. As opposed to just talking about it. And if I can be of help in that, well and good. They reckon that thirty or forty million people are going to watch this show. Anyway, this is the way it's done now. And O'Brien is a hell of a guy."

"I'm glad you don't hate it," she said.

"Well, it's a technique like everything else. I was stiff in the beginning, but then I warmed up and it went off all right. The trick is to ignore the camera. Just talk as if the camera wasn't there."

"Did Charles O'Brien tell you that?"

"No, I just picked it up. It happened. If you work it right you can blot out the camera and the lights and the people who go with it. The paraphernalia, the cameras. Out of your mind. They take my notes and put them on a teleprompter, and when I fall short of words I can look at that and get a clue. But I almost never have to. I've one or two tricks of my own, and if those fail then I can sneak a look. It's the damnedest gadget, I wish I had one at the briefings. But the cameraman on the project, Joe somebody, said it was the best thing he'd ever filmed."

"Darling!"

The captain smiled and shrugged. "That's what he said. I don't know if he meant it, but he said it."

"*What* did you talk about?"

"He's supposed to be a great cameraman." The captain sighed. "One of the best." He watched his wife sitting in the armchair, absently leafing through a woman's magazine, her feet tucked up under her. Her habit in the evenings, after dinner. The television set was on, its sound turned low. He wanted to tell her more about the filming, the look of the cemetery at dusk, the language the technicians used. He saw her looking at him, puzzled.

"What did you talk about?" she repeated. "What is it that you're saying to them?"

He smiled. "This and that." She nodded. "The Medal of Honor, one or two other things. You know."

"Your army life."

"My life period," he said.

"Yes," she said. Then: "I think it's wonderful."

"Well, I wasn't going to mention this. But O'Brien said the same thing after he saw the rushes."

"I guess I'll have to watch the show," she said.

"How does your wife fit into this life?"

"She's a good wife."

"But how does she feel about the war?"

"Well, that's my job. Like most women, she doesn't like war. But she understands that soldiering is my business. She understands that." The captain paused for a moment and looked to his left, down the long line of gravestones. The light was failing over the Potomac, and he could faintly hear the sounds of traffic on Shirley Highway. A private jet inbound to National Airport descended over the cemetery. "She was very proud when I got the Medal of Honor. Very, very proud." He raised his voice slightly: "We never talked about the circumstances of it. I guess she read about that in the papers, and of course there were several different versions. It was pretty hairy. This is not to say anything against the nation's press, but they were like the blind man and the elephant — you know? She never asked me directly about it, though, and I never told her."

"She never *asked* you?"

"No." The captain shook his head.

"Well, what did she say when you got the news?"

"She said it was wonderful. There were ceremonies, you know, and interviews and so forth." The captain described the parade in his hometown, the rows of Boy Scouts and American legionnaires. The mayor, the members of the city council. And the ceremonies at the White House, where the President himself read the citation.

The reporter muttered to the assistant producer to make certain that the camera with the long lens was filming the captain. He wanted the camera to bring him into the middle distance, still a long shot but enough to make him visible, in profile among the gravestones. He motioned for the close camera to move back and give the captain room to walk.

"What did she say when the ceremony was over?"

"I don't remember. We had tea with the President and the secretary of the army, and then we went home. There were two others in the ceremony. One air force and one marine, as I recollect. Both noncommissioned officers."

"Did you wonder about that at all?"

"What? The noncoms?"

"No, no. Your wife. Let me read part of the citation right here." He heard the familiar words and phrases, formed in the stilted language of the military, "conspicuous gallantry . . . at great peril . . . took command." When the reporter was finished, the captain was confused. What did they want him to say? He was standing apart from them now, and the reporter had to raise his voice to be heard. The captain began an answer, talking rapidly.

"Sorry, Captain. You're talking too fast. Take your time. No rush."

"Well, she was concerned about my safety, of course. But this is all in retrospect, all after the fact. Like any wife whose husband is in a jam. And we were in one *serious* jam. She was happy that I got out of it, that's all. I don't think she concerned herself with the details, they were pretty grim. Why should she? By the time she heard about it, the action was over."

The reporter waited a moment before answering: "No reason at all."

"She's a damn fine wife."

The reporter was silent, letting the tape roll. He knew the long-range camera was focused on all of them, the camera and the lights, the captain standing a little apart. A tiny group of men on the grass among the gravestones, like a matador and his *cuadrilla*, the reporter thought. The captain looked solemn, the microphone would pick up his breathing. This was a long minute, a long still scene: the reporter stared at the captain, who had turned his profile to the camera. This soldier had picked up the tricks very quickly. But the reporter was surprised to notice that the captain's hands were trembling.

"Do you talk about it at all now?"

"No."

"I see. It's a dead-letter issue, then."

"It was a couple of years ago, more than that. It was three springs ago. The afternoon of the twenty-second of April. Three in the afternoon. I was going to write her about it, all the details, but then I didn't. As I've explained, it was all available in the newspapers."

"Accurate and inaccurate."

"Mostly the latter," the captain said with a smile.

"What did they get wrong?" The reporter wanted to put the interview back on the track. He wanted to get the captain back to his wife.

"It's hard to explain, sir." The captain paused, and shifted his feet. "It's very confusing, a battle. Nobody ever gets all of it. The after-action reports are only half-right, even the people who are there know only their own part. It's all just details."

"Well, your own part then. Just that part."

"It's a long time ago."

"But it must have been a critical moment. In your life," the reporter said, and added: "And your wife's."

"Well, she wasn't in the war."

The reporter was silent now, knowing from experience that the captain would have to speak. The camera and the lights were intimidating. It was impossible to ignore them, for the same reason that it was impossible to ignore a ringing telephone. The experts were able to avoid it, but this captain was no expert. Knowing that the cameras were rolling, an amateur would feel forced. The reporter decided to keep still, to wait patiently until the captain picked it up again.

"This was my second tour."

Silence.

"I was commanding a company then."

Silence.

"There were a hundred and forty of us, it was an understrength company. This was in the highlands. Near a river,

I never could pronounce the name of it. Our mission was to sweep through a valley."

Silence.

"It developed there was a whole lot of enemy dug in along the trail. Which was mined and booby-trapped, although we didn't find that out until later. It was at the end of a long day. Very hot."

The reporter was giving instructions to the far camera, to move in on the captain very slowly. A millimeter at a time, bring him into close focus so slowly he would fill the screen before the audience was aware of it. No voice-over this time, he wanted it entirely natural; he wanted the actual scene, as the captain was speaking the words.

"We bumped them and they hit us."

Silence.

"We call that a meeting engagement."

The captain smiled and the reporter turned away, as if he were speaking to the cameraman.

"As you read in the citation, we lost about two dozen killed and wounded. We were out on our own, there wasn't anybody else. There was just our unit and theirs. Might've been on the moon, or any other uninhabited or undiscovered place. I couldn't raise headquarters on the radio, so we had to stick it out with no help and no advice. For about an hour we were orphans."

There was another long silence, while the captain put his thoughts in order. The reporter nudged the assistant producer and whispered in his ear, "hands." The other nodded and told the cameraman to focus in tight on the captain's hands, which were fluttering at his side.

"They lost upwards of fifty men, when the air strikes and the artillery were over. I'd crawled into one of their bunkers with my RTO and we directed the fight from there."

"So you were out on your own," the reporter said.

"I've explained that."

"What did you think about during that time? Did you think about home, or . . ."

"I was trying to stay alive."

"Yes, but during the pauses . . ."

"There weren't any," the captain said.

"So you didn't think about anything other than your position, where you were, and what your job was." The way the reporter phrased it, the question sounded critical.

"I thought about my wife," the captain said stiffly.

The reporter smiled, he thought he had it now. He wanted to move in gently, without alarming the captain.

"She was living where?"

"In Hawaii. We had an apartment there."

"And you'd been apart how long on this tour?"

"About six months. I was due for some leave."

They were taking simultaneous pictures now, tight shots from the close camera and the panorama from the camera on the bluff. They would edit later. The reporter had motioned the captain away from the gravestone, and now he was standing alone about twenty yards distant.

"Yes, it was about six months," the captain said.

The reporter could feel the moment moving away again. The soldier had his hands in his pockets and was staring at the ground. "Was this an inspiration for you?" the reporter asked. "Knowing you'd be off on home leave soon?"

The captain shrugged.

"Knowing that you'd be able to see your wife in Hawaii or wherever?" He signaled the close camera to move in tight, to fill the lens with the face of the captain. He wanted the camera to focus on the man's eyes. "When you thought about your wife, what exactly did you think about?" The reporter watched his man very carefully, he was working as delicately as a surgeon. But he was almost there. The reporter pressed again: "Did you think about . . ."

"I thought about survival," the captain said.

Silence.

"My survival."

"And?" the reporter asked quickly. But the soldier said nothing. He was standing at attention, still as stone, staring levelly ahead of him. His jaw muscles were tight. "And then what, *Captain?*"

He seemed in a trance, his eyes were blurred and in motion. He turned to the reporter and opened his eyes wide, as if seeing him for the first time. He shook his head and murmured, "Nothing." The reporter waited, gambling. A moment passed, then the captain straightened. It seemed a very great effort for him to do so. He looked at the camera and smiled crookedly. He talked directly at it now, as if it were a human being. "I killed half a dozen men. It was an action that was over in two hours and a half, and we had help from a lot of fine people. We damaged the enemy. After we got hit, they were outstanding. They put in air and artillery, and then they flew in some choppers to take us out. That was all there was to it. They flew us back to base camp. That's the end of the story."

"But you —"

"There's no more to it," the captain said.

"But you were talking —"

"Nothing," said the captain.

The reporter nodded slowly and motioned for the assistant producer to cut the far camera. There was no need for it now, they had all they could use. They had more than enough for a dozen special programs. He had been on the edge of something, and he'd almost made it good; but now it was gone for keeps. This surprised him, and he was not often surprised. But the captain had slipped the hook.

He turned away to say a word to the assistant producer, and then looked back at the captain. He was still standing, his profile to the camera, staring down the long row of graves, talking quietly. His voice was smooth and steady, the voice of a confident soldier. He was standing at ease, one hand in his pants pocket, the other resting lightly on a weathered marble tombstone. The captain was ramrod straight in the spine, and as the reporter looked at him he could see a small, tight smile on his lips. What a son of a bitch, the reporter thought; what an arrogant, insensitive son of a bitch. Then he nodded at the assistant producer to get the far camera rolling again. The captain evidently had more that he wanted to say.

The Brigadier General
and the Columnist's Wife

THE columnist had been active in his trade for thirty years. He was one of those who had made his reputation in World War II — *war two*, he called it now — marching across France with the Ninth Infantry Division. It was in France with the division that he met Hemingway, who took a fancy to him. The two shared foxholes and danger and, according to at least one contemporary account, a woman. When acquaintances asked the columnist about Hemingway, he would shrug his shoulders and say very little. War two was a wonderful experience, and the columnist wanted to keep it to himself.

After the war the columnist's reputation grew. He spent the late 1940s in Greece and China, and in 1950 he was evacuated from Korea with a bullet hole in his left shoulder. The authorities set him up in a private room in an army hospital in Japan, so he could continue to write his column. He read the dispatches in the morning and composed his column in the afternoon, writing it with his good hand on a portable typewriter. The wound became infected, and the columnist spent six weeks in the army hospital.

One day in September the chief surgeon brought a movie star in to see him; she was making a tour of the hospital with a USO troupe. She stayed for drinks and dinner and then she stayed for the night and in a month they were married, quite privately, in Kyoto. Acquaintances were stunned; the columnist was then forty; the movie star was thirty, and at the top of her trade. The acquaintances gave the marriage six months, but they were wrong. It lasted two years and supplied the columnist with a fund of stories on which to dine. In the property settlement, the movie star was awarded the mansion they had occupied in Holmby Hills. The columnist said good riddance; he had called the place *Berchtesgaden*.

The columnist and the movie star had divided their time between New York, Washington, and Los Angeles. Now the columnist returned full time to Washington and resumed his military writing with vengeance. But the 1950s was a bleak period, for the wars were small and of little account. Nig-nog wars, the columnist called them; gratuitous insurgencies in the Middle East and the Orient, squalid little generals' coups in Latin America. The columnist returned from his trips depressed: he said he was too old to backpack with the infantry; now he could concentrate on grand strategy. His editors were disappointed, for the columnist had no equal in the description of violent combat.

So he turned to strategy and took six months to refresh his memory on that subject. He went through the commentaries of Caesar and Marcus Aurelius and the memoirs of Foch, the contemporary accounts of Liddell Hart, and much more that was less well known. It was in the midst of his book on grand strategy that he met Caroline, a quiet Washington young woman with no military background at all. The columnist was instantly enchanted and courted her with the single-mindedness that had been his trademark in the war: he took her with him on lectures, and once to France, where they spent a week with one of his old Resistance friends, now a distinguished publisher. With the publisher in tow, the columnist returned to the Normandy beachhead, where he embarked on an eight-hour exegesis of the assault and the fortifications, the manner in which the battle proceeded, and the blunders. So many blunders. At one point the Frenchman and Caroline were in tears together, listening to the columnist describe a repeated assault against an entrenched enemy gun position. The publisher devoted a page or two of his memoirs to the incident, describing it as "extraordinary, an afternoon of inspiration."

The columnist treated Caroline as a singular object of art, a serene and delicate event. Then forty-five, he married her in a ceremony in his house in Georgetown. The ceremony was large, the reception small; fifty guests, most of them journalists and military men, a few movie people, Washington lawyers. Caroline was dazzled, perhaps in part because of her age. She was nineteen.

The columnist's acquaintances were amazed at the change in their friend. He lost weight and returned to his column with a new zeal; his intelligence, always formidable, broadened and deepened. His book on strategy was wonderfully reviewed, and it was a rare week when one of his observations was not quoted in the national press or on television. He and his adoring wife were fixtures at the White House during that period, "both of them handsome as box tops," a gossipist wrote, chic together in a way that a very successful man and a beautiful young woman are chic. His interests widened: always bored with domestic politics, he covered the 1956 election campaign as if it were the breaching of the Rhine. On a tip from a family friend, he wrote a series of articles on conflict of interest within the Eisenhower Administration that won him a Pulitzer Prize. And canceled all further White House invitations. He was more pleased with that than with the other. The columnist disdained honors, believing them beneath him. But the Pulitzer came at the right time and caused numerous magazine "profiles." Suddenly the columnist found himself a celebrity. He had always been "known," his name recognized by anyone who carefully read newspapers. But now he was likely to be interviewed at airports, and in the spring sought for honorary degrees. A television network offered him a large fee to do a five-minute commentary three times a week. Pressed for cash, the columnist accepted, and the commentary became one of the ornaments of television in the late 1950s.

While his interests did widen to include politics and economics, his preoccupation remained the army. Strategy, tactics, ways of war, military personalities. When a young major he had known in Korea was promoted to brigadier general, the columnist wrote him a long letter of congratulations; then he asked him around to dinner, not once but half a dozen times. The columnist "talked him up" (as he said) and wrote two glowing accounts of the officer's heroics in Korea almost a decade before: in fact, it had been the major who was responsible for the columnist's war wound; he had encouraged him to accompany a dangerous patrol. Far from ending the friendship, the incident strengthened it. A brigadier general three months, the officer found himself named secretary to the joint staff.

The columnist was pleased with his coup for his protégé, although he did not speak of it to anyone save Caroline. Gradually, in the late 1950s and early 1960s, he discarded the other interests and came back to the military. He refreshed his memory on weaponry and orders of battle, and commenced to cultivate those new officers who had made their reputations in his absence. His analysis of the British army, written in 1958, stands as a model of its kind; his inquiry into the temperament of military leaders, *Eminent Warriors*, is now a standard text at the command and general staff school at Fort Leavenworth. He hastened to Cyprus and Kenya and Malaya and Indochina and all the other places where there was fighting. These were brave moves on the part of the columnist, because the public then, as now, was bored with military affairs. In the early 1960s, there were no wars of consequence.

In Washington there are people who remember, and can cite, the column that signaled the decline. Except that it is always a different column. Acquaintance A is entirely convinced that it began with the vendetta against the secretary of state. There were twenty-one straight columns, seven weeks of columns, each one attacking the intelligence and integrity of the secretary, a harmless New York lawyer, long active in the Council on Foreign Relations. Acquaintance B is equally certain that it began six months later, with the column on farm price-supports. What was odd about this column was that it had been ten years since anyone cared about farm price-supports, and the article itself was incomprehensible. At the time, it caused more laughter than dismay; readers assumed that lines had been dropped somewhere in the transmission, and the copy had become garbled. Acquaintance C, with considerably more authority, is certain that it came later still, the column that everyone now calls "the war column." It was quite simply a celebration of war, of blood and of killing, of "the cleansing nature of armed combat." In it, the columnist announced his theory of war and human progress; that is, the one was impossible (he used the word "indispensable") without the other. It was a circular theory, working both ways. Appalled, his acquaintances sought out the columnist's wife: what had happened to him? Tight-lipped, she shook her head, refusing to explain. The columnist's wife, clearly upset, would blandly change the subject and go on to other things.

The war column appeared on a Monday, and that night the columnist and his wife had eighteen in to dinner. There was the usual array, journalists, a senator, two lawyers, a visiting academic, an intelligence official, and the brigadier general, the columnist's old friend. The senator knew the columnist best and over drinks put the question to him. Immediately the party fell silent, listening.

The senator dispensed with all preliminaries and asked straight off: "What the hell was that column about this morning?"

The columnist smiled.

"Damnedest bilge I've ever read."

The columnist selected a canapé from a tray.

"I think it goes beyond all bounds."

"*De mortuis nil nisi bonum,*" the columnist replied, which explained nothing and satisfied no one.

There were other columns after that, and in Washington

these had the effect of heightening interest in his work. He was the most closely watched writer in town. Between explosions there would be a series of reasonable, often deft, sometimes brilliant columns about missiles or new tanks or aircraft, with occasional skillful excursions into the national economy. But the television network, fearful of slander or worse, canceled his contract. For his acquaintances, picking up the newspaper in the morning was like picking up a hand grenade. On the morning of the sixth of June, 1962, appeared the most alarming column of all. It was a movie review. The film was an adaptation of a celebrated novel of the period, a novel written around the Korean War. The costar was the columnist's ex-wife, and the last line of the column read: "Anyone venturing an interest into the noblest endeavors of our time must witness this film. Miss Harrison's performance is as luminous as a star, and as moving as death itself."

The columnist and his wife did not have friends the way other people had friends. They had companions, acquaintances, chums. Their house was a salon, and people felt free to stop by. The caterers arrived every Saturday and left again on Wednesday morning, after four nights of parties. In the beginning, Caroline found this exciting. The columnist knew everyone in town, and introductions to anyone he did not know were easily arranged. His brief connection with the movie industry had given him a wide acquaintance in the theater, so the weekend parties were interesting and vivid. The columnist presided over these affairs with style and consideration. He arranged the seating (always placing his wife next to the most interesting, rather than the most prominent, guest), and if conversation fell, he pumped it up again, with an anecdote or outrageous war story. It was in this way that Caroline fell to talking a good deal with the brigadier general; both of them knew the anecdotes and the war stories by heart.

New acquaintances were conducted on a tour through the study, a room which Caroline called "the armory." It was filled with military artifacts and photographs of the columnist in army fatigues: with Bradley in Europe, with de Castries in Indochina, with the movie star by his hospital bed in Japan. His favorite photograph was of himself in a trench. In the photo he is intense and scowling, squatting in the dirt with his typewriter on his knees. The trench is filled with dead.

The columnist's weekend parties became unpopular not long after the appearance of the movie review, owing to his habit of conducting strange monologues in the early hours of the morning. He would address the two or three stragglers, pulling his chair up close to the edge of the rug in front of the fire. And reprise the wars. He did it quietly, in blackest humor, precise minute-by-minute reconstructions of forgotten engagements, so many dead in the first five minutes, so many wounded in the first ten. Their names and ages and ranks. He would describe the setting of the battle in the larger context of the war, whichever war it was. He once saw a man shot in the heart, and took to describing that with such care and loving attention to detail that once a guest walked out of his house, physically ill. He would speak of the camaraderie during wars, the closeness of men and women; the community of it. But he would not expand on that. He thought of the century as a gigantic hecatomb. But exhilarating, he'd say. And war two the best war of all, the most violent, the most profound. Late at night he would talk about the major, now a brigadier general, in the same breath as Guderian or Patton. Occasionally, he would seem to be confused over the nature of his wounds. Just a kid then, he'd say, just a kid. The major, he'd add, "my priest."

Every year the parties ended on October one, and resumed again late in December. This was the period when the columnist took his trip, to view for himself the various wars then in progress. There were always one or two, somewhere around the world. His reputation was such that he could secure interviews with anyone, and each trip included an example of his old style. It was a visit to a field hospital or a guerrilla command in the bush or something of that sort, and it was then that his prose took flight, there that he was most comfortable and in command. He'd be gone a month or six weeks, then would meet Caroline in Athens or Cairo or Madrid. He would write a month's columns in advance, and they would take a trip: the Pyramids, the bullfights, a tour of Berlin, and once a magical two weeks on the Trans-Siberian Railway. In the beginning, he was a wonderful guide, because he had been everywhere once and could reminisce about the old days. About Segovia in 1938 or Kasserine in 1942 or the time he went on the bombing mission from the north of Scotland in 1944. Tourane in 1952.

"Is there any place where you haven't been in a war?" Caroline asked him on one of the early trips.

He thought a moment, then shook his head.

"No place at all?"

"New Zealand," he said finally.

"Let's go there."

"Dull country," he said. "What's the point?"

"I'd like it so much."

"Oh, sure," he said, but they never went.

It was during one of these absences, in the period before she was to join him in a capital somewhere, that the columnist's wife had the affair with the brigadier general. The affair was reminiscent of another, and in the columnist's younger days he would have laughed about it, perhaps with Hemingway or Capa. The brigadier general came by the Georgetown house one afternoon with a manila envelope full of documents. He stayed for drinks and dinner and then for the night.

No one knows what animated the affair, nor what kept it going. Caroline had seemed happy, if distracted; there was always an exquisite poignance about her, as if her life were lived on the edge of something, perhaps exile. Often at parties she'd stare at her husband across the table, desperately protective of him — his vitality, his easy dominance, his pride, and of course, his prejudice. On the evenings he talked about war she would retire to another corner, but there is no evidence that she ever abandoned him in any traditional way. So young, she loved and admired him; but she was frightened by things she was unable to understand. There is a single written record from the period, and for obvious reasons it must be read with skepticism. It is a novel, a *roman à clef*, written by the columnist's former secretary. The novel was published in 1963, enjoyed a brief success of scandal in Washington, then died. Two picturesque chapters purport to describe the love affair between Caroline and the brigadier general. One passage suggests the entire dreadful book.

They lay in each other's arms, apprehensive, as if watched by the photographs on the walls. The general's uniform lay crumpled beside the couch, the single star on his epaulet lit by the soft light of the room. It was as if *he* were there with them. His presence dominated the room.

"Do it again," she said.

And he did, as if on command.

"Doesn't he do it at all?"

"Oh, yes." She seemed quite appalled by the inference.

"Well..."

"It isn't that. He's only fifty-three, he's done —"

"I see."

The brigadier general was a plainspoken man, and he did not understand why he was there, on the couch with her. He was enjoying it, but he didn't understand it. But then, he didn't understand the columnist either.

"Why me then?"

"Well, you were there in Korea. His friend."

"I still don't get it."

She smiled, and pointed at the pictures, all of them. The pictures from all the wars. She was pointing at the pictures and laughing. Her laughter grew in volume, louder and louder until she was hysterical and finally she collapsed in his arms, sobbing and crying for him to do it again.

The author of the *roman à clef* didn't understand what it was about either, because the chapter ends one paragraph later. Further on in the book there is an account of what happened when the columnist found out about the affair, but that account has no value because the secretary by then had quit and was in New York selling an outline of her book.

The affair with the brigadier general began in late 1962 and lasted through most of 1963. The columnist returned from his trip in November, a month ahead of schedule, ill with fever contracted in central Africa. The trip had not been a success anyway, and he took leave from his column and of course never resumed it. The column just trailed away, as he did.

Friends found him one afternoon in his study, the armory, staring blackly at a thick loose-leaf folder. The folder contained hundreds, perhaps a thousand, names. They were carefully written, three names to a page, in the columnist's thin script. He refused to speak, and for a time no one could decipher what the names meant; they were names in numerous languages. It should have been obvious, but it was not, until Caroline explained. They were the names of dead, she said. Companions, acquaintances, chums. Soldiers, war correspondents, various political people. The columnist was seated at his desk, staring at the list, defiance on his face. He gripped the loose-leaf folder with such strength that it was impossible to pry it from his hands. It stayed with him, part of him.

That is close to the end of the story. The brigadier general was transferred from the Pentagon to Fort Carson, his career in ruins. Caroline followed him there, stayed six months, then returned to the house in Georgetown. The general went on to the Far East, and when last heard of he was still there. No one has heard anything of Caroline except a rumor that she was in the Far East, too. Though not, of course, with him.

Simpson's Wife

HE always finished dressing before she did and slipped down to the kitchen to make a drink before they went out. Now he was leaning on the armoire in their bedroom, the drink in his hand, watching her fix her face in the bathroom. He saw her once removed from across the room, looking into the mirror at her reflection as she pouted and grimaced, arranging her eye makeup and hair. He sipped his drink and stood quite still, staring straight into the mirror.

". . . will you try to do that? You can do it."

"Ummmm," she said, talking around a pin in her mouth.

"He'll talk to you."

She nodded.

"It's causing me real problems, as you well know. Or maybe you don't. Anyway, if I lean on him it'll just antagonize him. Those bastards, you ask them for the time of day and they think you're trying to repeal the First Amendment. Still, I don't know what he's after. What he wants."

"Sim?"

"It's the third day in a row he's been on my back. This little thing of mine just isn't worth all that space. No one cares about it except me and a few friends. Hell, it's still in committee; it hasn't even been *reported* yet. Little pissant, just affects a few guys. Someone's put him up to it, and I don't know who. The tax laws're so damned complicated now, a man can't do business. Now, that's the truth of the matter: a legitimate businessman cannot operate."

"Will you hook me up?"

"I got two calls from home today on it, guys wanting to know what was up. What's Baxter on your back for? It's lousy publicity, and it comes at the wrong time. Someone's put him up to it, I repeat. OK, you're hooked."

"It'd be easier if you put down the drink."

"So if you talk to him, I might know what's going on. What he wants."

"I'll talk to him."

"You're a sweetheart."

"What do you want me to say?"

"I'll leave that to your judgment. You can ask him what he thinks he's doing. Tactfully, of course; casual. Why he's interested."

"That's very tactful."

"Well, you know."

"Sure."

"The goddamned fag," Simpson said.

They put the top down on the Pontiac, and Simpson's wife drove. The night was balmy, the congressman took off his white jacket and laid it carefully on the back seat; he handed his wife a silk scarf for her hair. Simpson was satisfied, feeling good, the warm night air spilling over the windshield and ruffling his hair. They cruised slowly up Massachusetts Avenue, the tires of the Pontiac squeaking on the warm pavement.

"Do you need any money?"

"Money?"

"Your account. Is your account full?"

"Sure. I suppose it is."

"Well, I just wondered if it was low."

"It isn't low, Sim."

"I was just wondering."

"You can put in another thousand if you want. I can use some things for the house. I can buy another chaise, and a rug for the dining room. Maybe a summer coat for myself. One or two of those things, not all of them."

"I'll have Sheila put some money in the account tomorrow."

They drove in silence for a bit, past St. Alban's School and the National Cathedral and up Massachusetts Avenue into Spring Valley.

"What's the cast of characters tonight?"

Simpson thought a moment and named one senator (Whyte), two lawyers from the large downtown firms, the British DCM, and the journalist, her friend Baxter. Simpson knew all the moves; they would have two cocktails on the porch, then drift inside for dinner. They would talk soberly about the campaign, who was up, who was down; the political errors of one candidate, the money troubles of another. Baxter would lead the conversation, quoting from his columns no doubt. Simpson had been keeping in reserve one or two new facts to reveal, and these would be interesting, particularly to Whyte.

Simpson's wife was smiling. "Billy Baxter. I can never get over it. When I first knew him . . ."

"He's still a *nothing*," Simpson said.

"You don't say," she said.

"You give them nine square inches of print, and they think they're Arnold Toynbee. Or the avenging angel."

"Billy Baxter," she said.

"Well, he's bitten off too much this time. I can handle him. On the other hand, he may have shot his wad. He may be all finished now."

"Billy was always known for his persistence," she said. Simpson grunted.

"It'll be good to see him again."

"Don't let me get stuck with Mary Whyte, OK?"

"You save me from the fool she's married to, the senator."

" 'The Fool,' as you call him, is one of the five or six most powerful men in the United States."

She smiled and drove on. She liked the night, with its sounds and what she believed was its promise. She thought that June was gorgeous in Washington, the flowers in bloom and the night air so soft and tropical, so sensual. She was sexier in the summer than in the winter, and there was no satisfactory explanation for it. She thought that it had to do with lying naked between cool white sheets; she refused to buy an air conditioner for the bedroom. She felt the wind in her face and drove very slowly to Tilden Street, then turned and slid the car next to the curb. Simpson was up and out and standing impatiently on the sidewalk as she extricated herself from behind the wheel, after first checking in the rear-vision mirror to see that her lipstick was on straight and her hair neatly done. She smiled to herself, because she saw she was blushing.

After dinner, Baxter stood in a corner of the living room, talking with Mary Whyte. Simpson's wife took a demitasse from the silver tray and moved to join them. The three talked for five minutes, and then Mary Whyte left to join the others. A butler moved softly around the room, offering liqueurs and Scotch.

"How are you, Bill?"

"The better for seeing you. It's been a long time. You're looking *very* well tonight."

"It's the air," she said.

"I thought it might be the summer."

"Maybe that, too."

Baxter laughed; he'd known Simpson's wife for fifteen years, since college. They walked away from the others and stood in the doorway to the back porch.

"Bill, will you tell me? Who's the one sitting over *there*, the one next to our hostess. I didn't catch his name."

Baxter slowly turned around, as if he were looking for something lost. Then he turned back.

"That's Bergen."

"He's a lawyer?"

"Well, not exactly. I suppose he has a law degree somewhere. But actually he introduces people." He watched her face break into a smile, as he knew it would. Now he could string the story out a little, and they would have some fun.

"Who? What do you mean?" Simpson's wife laughed. "What is he, a headwaiter? A professional greeter?"

"In a way." Baxter lit a cigarette and smiled. "Look, a guy wants to get together with another guy, and maybe it's inconvenient for the one guy to call the other. Perhaps, for some odd reason, that's awkward. Well, Bergen gets the parties together. A guy calls him and then he calls the other guy. Perhaps there's a financial transaction first. Anyway, he has a house that he uses for the introductions."

Simpson's wife was amused; she found something new in Washington every day. Washington was not New York or San Francisco; it was too public in too many ways. But there were other compensations. People from the outside thought it was glamorous and exciting to dine with the secretary of state or the Senate majority leader. But that wasn't it at all. Those people were bores. What enchanted her about Washington were the Baxters and the Bergens, men who were back in the woodwork, men with no specific authority or title, but the men who made the town go. Toads, she called them. An hour with Bergen was worth an hour with anybody, with the possible exception of Baxter, whose life was complicated *beyond belief*, and who knew everything. He was one of the reasons she loved Washington and would never leave. The parties she went to, so serene and unselfconscious on the outside, and so gloriously intricate once you knew the secrets. Simpson's wife saved secrets like other women saved string.

"So he gets men together," she said.

"That's right."

"In his house. Then he leaves the room?"

"Sometimes yes, sometimes no. Depends on what he has to contribute. Sometimes he contributes a good deal. Often Bergen is the nominee, for one party or the other. Once — oh, it is doubtless an exaggeration — he is said to have negotiated with himself. He worked it so he was the nominee for two men. These were men who would've found it awkward to meet in person. The negotiations were held at such long range that he was able to . . . sell himself each to the other. Turn and turn about, as you might say. Then he cut himself in for a percentage of the deal both ways."

"And was everyone satisfied?"

"Very," Baxter said.

"Would there be another name for that?" Simpson's wife was looking Baxter in the eye, suppressing her laughter. He was the only man she knew who took her seriously enough to be droll. It was not a town of wits, and Baxter was very special in that way. He was very easy with her now. "What do you think it would be?"

Baxter appeared very grave, his hands went to his temples and he thought. "Perhaps . . . fixer?"

"Would you call him a fixer, Bill?"

"I think I would."

"Then so will I," Simpson's wife said.

They were silent for a minute, looking at each other and grinning. Baxter thought he would save the specifics that he knew about Bergen. Simpson's wife would want to hear them later.

"What are you now, thirty-five?"

"Six," she said. "Six last week. Married fifteen years, and in the prime of my time."

"It's not fifteen years."

He looked and sounded so serious that she laughed and imitated his voice. "Yes, it's fifteen years."

"I'll be damned."

"Well, he's been on the Hill for twenty. Controlling that committee for three. He *does love* that committee; do you think there's anything unnatural about it?"

"It's a very beautiful committee. Rich, too."

She moved toward him and grinned. "It's the only thing he does control."

"Well, that spoils my compliment. It might make you think that I had some undercover, hidden, *ulterior* motive . . ."

"I wouldn't think of it, Bill." She began to laugh. "You go right ahead and say it, whatever it is. I hope you were going to say that I was beautiful, too."

"As a matter of fact, I was going to say that you have no competition anywhere. And was going to add that, unlike the committee, you are not dumb."

"Gee, thanks. I like the dumb part."

"Wonderful-looking. Brainy. Transcendent."

"Careful," she said.

"That, too."

"Well, isn't it a fair trade? He has the committee. I have Washington. We have what we want." She shrugged.

"I hope you had a birthday party."

"Well, a delegation was in from the district, so instead of a birthday party we had a buffet. They were schoolteachers, wonderfully interesting, really. Science teachers, as I recall. The delegation was . . . so interesting. It was very hot last week, you'll recall."

"Particularly the nights," Baxter said.

"Yes, those. The days, too."

"You know, Sim knows Bergen pretty well."

"I had a hunch that he might," she said.

Simpson was on the couch, talking to Bergen and Whyte. He said a good deal more than he'd meant to, and his lis-

teners were attending to the words. He watched his wife
and Baxter in the porch doorway; she was almost as tall as
he was. He saw her touch his arm, and then laugh. Baxter
leaned forward and whispered something into her ear, and
she laughed again, loudly; she was laughing too loudly.
Scandal, Simpson thought, they were talking scandal. He
could tell by the way his wife laughed, throwing her head
back and running her hand through her hair. The journalist
turned toward their couch, then looked away.

"Sim?"

It was Bergen. Whyte had left to fix a drink.

"What's Baxter on your ass for?"

Simpson shrugged and muttered an obscenity. He didn't
want to talk about Baxter; there was nothing Bergen could
do about him. He would leave Baxter to his wife.

"Are we on for Thursday?"

"We are," Bergen said.

"Are you meant to be there as well?"

"I can be there if you want me to be there, always on
the proviso that it isn't inconvenient for the others. This
can't be clumsy in any way."

"I think it would be a hell of a good thing. I want to
make it absolutely clear to our friends what can and cannot be done. And I think it would be appropriate for you
to be there. As the disinterested party, in case any questions
come up. These guys have a habit of juicing promises."

"*D'accord*," Bergen said.

"But if that goddamned Baxter keeps it up, there won't
be any *d'accord*, so you'd better remember that."

"The others asked me about him."

"You can tell them that Mr. Baxter will cease and desist.

After tonight." He wondered if his wife had had a chance
to work in close, to find out what Baxter was doing and
where he was getting his information from. Now Bergen
was asking him another question, and Simpson refocused
to answer it. He thought that sometimes he did not understand his wife, who could have a very good time with a
bloody fag. She looked to be enjoying herself.

"What are you up to now, Bill?"

"You know damned well what I'm up to."

"You've been a little hard on Sim lately. Poor baby, he
can hardly sleep."

"Poor Sim."

"He thinks you want something from him. That you've
got an angle and you're not letting on what it is."

"Baxter with an angle? Improbable."

She smiled; she knew that when he spoke in the third
person he was concealing something. It was an old habit of
journalism. "Sim thought that maybe you wanted something and he could get it for you."

"If I get one more break, I'll get the Pulitzer Prize."

She said quietly, "Is it that serious?"

"That serious," he said.

"Well, if you want an introduction . . ."

He smiled at her.

"I'm here." She paused, and leaned toward him. "Look,
Bill. I'd not meant to get into that at all. Really, I meant
your life. How things were. Any happier now . . . than
then?"

"Some," he said.

"Well, I won't say the obvious things. We've talked

about it before, God knows." She smiled quickly. "Too much, maybe."

"Well, it's a varied life. As you know." He paused. "Then as now, it doesn't change a hell of a lot."

She nodded; he seemed to want to talk about it. She thought he was going to say something more and waited for it, and when he didn't there was dead space between them. "Where are you living?" she asked.

"Same house, near the cathedral. It's quiet. I planted a magnolia in my backyard. You're invited to see it. Very nice in the summertime, a drink in the backyard . . ."

She looked at him, hurt. "I know that."

"It's not much of a life. We had a better one, I think."

She was silent a moment. Then: "Sim's going back to the district next week, a ten-day visit. I'll be alone here, no obligations at all. He leaves on Tuesday, sometime in the morning. Come by that night. I'll cook dinner. Or the afternoon, if you like. Luscious," she said.

"I'd like that."

"You're free then?"

"Like the seasons, darling. Spring's ended, summer's here. Change, the meaning of life. We were always summer people. That's Washington; the people change but the town remains the same. We know all about that, don't we?"

She pressed: "What are you going to do about Sim?"

He looked at her, saw her blush.

"Bill?"

She touched his arm, he imagined the urgent softness of her fingers.

"You know damned well," he said, and they both laughed.

Noone

THE emotions of it were fairly straightforward, and I don't want to make too much of them in any case, either way. She was crying on the bed, or it sounded like crying, and I was in my rage at the doorway. I had said the words so many times in my head that when I said them out loud, they sounded false. I told her we were finished, and I was leaving. She told me to get out then, and I did. After I slammed the door, I couldn't hear her anymore. I stood for a moment in the street, then began to walk down Dent Place to Wisconsin Avenue. I was walking very quickly, head down, looking for a taxi. The regular Yellow would arrive at eight, but I didn't feel like waiting for half an hour. My knees were shaky and I kept to the inside of the sidewalk. Then I collected myself and slowed up. My briefcase swung in rhythm, my footsteps even on the sidewalk. Click click click click.

I arrived at my office in thirty minutes; only a few people were in. The receptionist, one or two others. My secretary followed me through the small offices to the large one, bearing a cup of coffee. She remarked on the weather, hot, and the day, heavy, and handed me the appointments list and waited.

"Is Noone in yet?" I asked.

"Noone's downtown this morning. Back at eleven."

I nodded, irritated.

"At eleven, then."

"Shall I telephone?"

"No need," I said.

My secretary made a small note on her stenographer's pad.

"And hold all calls."

There were two meetings that morning. We were having trouble with a transcript. I wanted State to agree to release an uncensored version of an ambassador's testimony, and State had refused. Can't conduct diplomacy in a fishbowl, the secretary said; not so much a fishbowl, more a muddy river, I replied. He smiled. I smiled. *No*, he said then, very politely, knowing he had the strength. The White House would back him, so the thing was hopeless. That was where Noone was now, at the State Department talking to their legislative man. Making everything as difficult as possible for them. Like everything else, it had its positives and negatives. I was getting solid publicity, and the cause was a good one, which it isn't always. But the dispute had gone on for a month, and people were tiring of it; some of my colleagues on the committee were tiring of it. Noone and I agreed that there should be one last press release, then forget it. An issue that became a bore was worse than no issue at all. But others had come in behind us, and the two meetings this morning were to let them down gently. To tell them we weren't marching anymore, at least at the head of the parade. This will sound fatuous, but it is true:

I have always tried never to let people down without warning them.

I have two offices, a public office and a private office. The public office is very large, with a huge mahogany desk in the center of an oval rug. The Capitol building is in the background, visible over my left shoulder through the windows. *What a wonderful view*, the visitors say, and I smile, *isn't it?* The desk belonged to my uncle when he was in the navy; it is a beautiful object. He bought it in Honduras and gave it to me when I first came here. The walls of this office are crowded with pictures of me and my family, me and politicians, me and military men, me and important constituents, and plaques with my name on them. They are commemorative, of this and that — Rotary, AUSA, AFL-CIO, the United Jewish Appeal. That sort of plaque. The other, smaller, office is personal and difficult to find in the maze of rooms in the Capitol. I have a small bar in the corner and an old Underwood typewriter and a bookshelf full of mystery novels. I have all of John D. MacDonald's sixty-odd books, plus Ian Fleming and Ross MacDonald and the others. No photographs, no plaques. A comfortable couch along one wall, leather chairs around the room, stand-up ashtrays, a government-issue desk. There is a seascape, a self-conscious impression of a slice of American coastline, Maine or California, Castine or Big Sur. I am in the smaller office now, waiting for Noone.

Gloria Noone is thirty-five, dark, compact, austere. She is divorced from a lawyer, and she pronounces her name "new-nee." Before she came to work for me she handled public relations for a television network, and although she is ten years younger than I am, I trust her judgment and her instincts. I trust her absolutely when it comes to dealing with the press. We did not get on well at first, owing mainly to her unfortunate habit of correcting the smallest mistakes. In the first interview we fell to talking, for some reason, about Iowa. I was making a point about redistricting.

"In the eight congressional districts of Iowa . . ." I began, but she interrupted.

"There are seven congressional districts in Iowa," she said, and named the congressmen.

It vexed me, and she saw that, and smiled. Of course then I had to hire her.

She knocks, is in the room.

"How did it go?"

"Fine," I say. She is talking about Nancy, but I am talking about the meetings this morning. "They took it very well. They seemed pleased that we had gone along as far as we did. Kudos. We get kudos."

"I'll get the last press release out right away." She looks at me, bland as warm milk. "As long as it went so well, we might think about a press conference."

I smile. Score one for Noone.

"I'll concentrate on the secretary personally."

"You do that."

"Pompous bureaucrat. Another Wall Street fool."

I laugh.

She puts up a hand; she's steady, resolute. "Senator, we will get the last *ounce* . . ."

Gloria Noone is talking, and I am looking over her head. The room is small, so comfortable. Sometimes I think she is a touch paranoid: she had it swept for bugs. Of course there were none. But the knowledge gives me a strange satisfaction. We are absolutely private in this room. We have a code word for it. The Vatican. I have only had the office for two years; they gave it to me after my tenth year in the Senate. But now I never talk about confidential matters in the large office; it is as if that office were ceremonial. Noone and I and sometimes Walter Mach go to the Vatican in the evenings. We do our business there, over a drink. They are for me the best hours in the day, sitting and planning; scheming, Noone says. The day they gave me the key to the office, Noone insisted that I go inside and talk in a normal voice, and she stayed outside with the door closed, listening. She wanted to be certain that nothing could be overheard in the corridor. And it can't be, even when you shout. The soundproofing is gorgeous. When I call her paranoid, Noone smiles and says she is cautious.

She is silent now, waiting for me.
"Well, we are quits."
"Sorry about that," she says. She manages to make it sound both sympathetic and ironic. So I can go either way, and she can follow.
We are both quiet for a moment, and I see her pick up a pencil and begin drawing boxes. One box is fastened to another, a series of boxes slanting down the white paper. She shifts on her chair, sighs, and rubs the flat of her hand along her cheeks. She pushes her hair back behind her ears, then she looks at me, a long moment.

"Nancy *is* staying."

I nod.

"And you're moving out."

I nod again.

"Well," she says. "Well." Noone is carefully inking in the boxes she has drawn, turning the paper as she does it. Now she is using a felt pen, and the ink is staining her fingers. She is unconscious of that. "I think," she says, "a short, blunt statement."

"The shorter the better."

"Two sentences," she says. She has stopped doodling altogether and is staring at the pad. Then she says, "Due to irreconcilable family differences, Senator and Mrs. Hayn . . ."

"Christ, no," I say. "Jesus Christ, no."

Noone shrugs; I am angry. But the anger does not concern her. She is silent for a moment, then tries another approach.

I am a fatalist, and that has served me well in politics. When I am in a tight spot I try to remember that life is capricious. Life is unfair, Jack Kennedy said. He could afford to say it, although he didn't believe it, really, and I do. He was more romantic than fatalist. Noone and I talked about fatalism once, just once. She said fatalism was for losers, and I laughed at her and called her Horatio Alger's mother. She looked at me as if I were insane.

There is a funny aspect to this. A month ago we looked for precedents and could find none. It isn't the sort of problem you can refer to the Legislative Reference Service, so Noone went personally to the morgue of the *Times*. I wanted her to find out how these problems had been handled in the past, specifically what was said, how it was explained. She drew a blank; perhaps the *Times* did not consider a politician's personal life news fit to print. So we are operating on our own instinct because it would have been awkward to ask questions, even of close friends. The place is like a sieve, Noone says.

She has tried two or three approaches now, and they are improving.

"Senator and Mrs. Tom Hayn have decided to seek a legal separation . . . well, no." She pauses, thinks, begins again. She is writing the statement as she recites it out loud. "Senator Thomas Hayn's office announced today that the senator and Mrs. Hayn . . . no." She begins again. "The senator *and his wife* have decided to seek a legal separation. Mrs. Hayn will continue to live in their Georgetown . . ."

"Uh, uh," I say.

"Oh, right. Dumb of me," she mutters. ". . . *their house in Washington, D.C.* The senator has moved . . ." She looks at me, her eyebrows up, inquiring.

"A downtown hotel," I say.

She smiles. "Right again. You should have my job."

I am thinking that after all I was right, and we should have prepared a statement in advance. But she argued against it, worried about a leak or the possibility of a misplaced piece of paper. We can work it up in two hours, she'd said. That would be a bad piece of paper to have lying around. I agreed finally. But now I don't see the need for all the detail, and I tell her that. I want a simple statement of fact. A one-line statement of fact.

"Tom, you have got to say something," she says. "You have got to give them more than the fact that you and Nancy are quits. So it has got to be in two sentences, and maybe three. This is not major news, but it is news. You have got to give them more than the blunt fact. If you don't, they'll know you're hiding something. They'll speculate."

"They'll speculate anyway."

"Of course. But if you give them something to chew on, the speculation will be built around that. I mean, it doesn't matter an awful lot what it is. What the extra fact is. I think that place of residence is the most neutral, and it fits; the impression is that you've nothing to hide. This is a family tragedy, politics be damned. That's the point we want to make."

Noone is at the bar. She fixes a martini for me and a Dubonnet for herself. She is lost in thought, worried now. The dining room has sent up sandwiches. There is no telephone, so we are quite alone. I smile when I think of that. It is the only office in Washington without a phone. If there is no telephone, Noone said, there will be no spur-of-the-moment, ill-considered calls. She prefers to conduct business face-to-face.

"How difficult is Nancy going to be?" She looks at me before she asks the next question, which I ignore. "How difficult was she this morning? Or was it last night?"

"I don't know," I say, which is the truth. We have been married for twenty years and have been in trouble the last ten. We are disconnected now, I don't know her feelings.

I am preoccupied with the immediate problem, which is the statement; I have lived with the other long enough to know it is insoluble. "I honestly don't know," I say. "Depends in part on that son of a bitch." I mention the name of Nancy's priest, and Noone smiles.

"Rasputin lives," she says.

"The hell with that, Gloria," I say.

She is back to business again.

"You are going to have to take gas."

"Unavoidable."

Noone is thinking, very quiet now. She is circling the subject, closing off the routes of access. She is very thorough. "Think about this," she says, leaning across the desk, concentrating on her drawing. She is very slowly inking in all the boxes. "It might be advantageous to leak it. It might be better to get the word out informally, to prepare the state for it. Then, in two or three days, make the official announcement." She looks up. "I don't think I would recommend this course, but it's one possibility and we ought at least to consider it."

So we talk, and finally I shake my head. "It's going to come as a hell of a surprise. Best to come from me, this office, officially. Better that than rumors for a week, followed by an announcement. They'll have me in bed with every woman in Washington anyway."

Noone nods gravely.

"Have the kids been told?"

"Nancy will do that," I say.

"But Tom junior's in Europe."

"She'll find a way."

"It'll be a surprise," she says.

"No, it won't."

"I mean in the state, and that's the bad part. The surprise."

"The Knights of Columbus," I say, grinning.

"The Holy Name Societies," she says.

"Monsignor Shaw," I say.

"The cardinal!" she cries.

And we both laugh.

Noone has prepared three statements, and I am reading them now. She gave them to me on one sheet of paper. They represent three different "spins," she said. This is how they look on the paper.

1. Senator and Mrs. Thomas Hayn have decided to seek a legal separation. Mrs. Hayn and their three children will continue to live at the family home in Washington, D.C. The senator has moved to a downtown hotel.

2. Senator Thomas Hayn's office announced with deep regret today that the senator and his wife have decided to seek a legal separation. Mrs. Hayn and their children will continue to live in the family home in Washington, D.C. The senator has moved to a downtown hotel.

3. Senator Thomas Hayn's office announced today that the senator and his wife, Nancy, have decided to seek a legal separation. Senator and Mrs. Hayn emphasized that their decision came most reluctantly and was made, finally, in the best interests of the family. Mrs.

Hayn and their three children will remain in the family home in Washington. The senator has moved to a downtown hotel.

I chose the third, naturally.

I am thinking of adding a single sentence: "There is no question of a divorce," but Noone is against it.

"The word looks terrible on paper and raises questions," she says.

"But it will be the first question they ask." I want to know how Noone intends to handle this particular inquiry.

"Of course. And I will answer it: 'There is no question of a divorce.' It will give them a second story, which they will have to have. There will be other questions about the children and their ages and Nancy and her age and so forth." She stops, smiles. "Thank God, there's no need to clear the statement with her."

I look up, startled. I hadn't thought of that.

"Not to worry," Noone says. "If she objects to a decision made 'in the best interests of the family,' then she's on the hook and you're off it. There's one thing in our favor. These stories are really awkward for them to pursue. The locals will be reluctant anyway, and you're not so famous that the nationals can really bird-dog it. If they do, it looks like a vendetta. Unless, of course, they smell real scandal." She smiles. "Then anything can happen."

"Thanks for all the good news," I say.

Noone is pleased; the statement has just the right tone, melancholy but dignified, she says. "When I talk to them privately tonight, I will stress the family tragedy aspects. I will not talk politics with them at all. I will tell them that you have gone away for a week. Tom, I am not going to close any doors." I return her stare. "It isn't unheard of. You will take gas, but attitudes have changed now. Even back home. I could foresee circumstances . . ." She does not finish the sentence. She types a clean copy of the statement on the old Underwood and leaves to return to the big office. Perhaps she is right; she is a smart woman. Times change. But I am feeling a little melancholy myself. If I'd been a Protestant, there'd be no trouble, or anyway less trouble. I think about that for a moment, then turn it around. If I'd been a Protestant, I would not be a senator.

The statement is typed and Xeroxed; it will be given to the press at eight or nine tonight. I leave the small office and walk across the street to the large one. Everyone is gone now, except for Noone. I look in on her and motion for her to follow me. She does, eagerly. We march into my office, and she places the call.

I talk to His Eminence.

His Eminence talks to me.

Because the question is lying there, palpable, a shadow between us, I try to reassure him. "John, I want to tell you personally that there is no question of any divorce or remarriage. Nor any third parties either. That is definite."

The old man grunts and says that he is glad to hear it.

But he doesn't believe it.

"You have let me down," he says. "You have let me down badly."

While I am talking, trying to explain the situation, I am

watching Noone. She is taut, excited; she seems to me like an athlete before a game. I cannot tell what she is thinking; her mouth is set in a hard thin line.

She'd insisted that Walter Mach not be brought into this, and I reluctantly agreed. I used to think that she and Walter were close, but now I am not so sure. She didn't want anyone brought into it; otherwise it would look like a council of war. "Bad atmospherics," she explained; "too political." She catches me looking at her and smiles slightly, distracted; she is perched on the edge of the big desk, her hand under one elbow, concentrating on the conversation. Her hair falls wonderfully over her face; she turns now, and her mouth and eyes are obscured. Her left leg swings free, describing a circle. The cardinal is silent, and there is nothing to do but say good-bye and hang up the telephone. I have known this cardinal since he was a bishop. I am in politics largely through the early patronage of this cardinal. We were friends.

Noone listens for two clicks, then puts down the extension phone.

"Pretty frosty," she says.

"Balls like ice cubes," I say absentmindedly.

"That bastard," she says. "With *his* record."

"Well, he is an old man."

"But he won't help."

"Why should he?" I ask.

We make six other calls after that.

I am walking down the Capitol steps. Very theatrical: it is raining softly, and wisps of steam rise from the still-hot pavement. The late-working secretaries are going home now, and I watch their bodies move. I am walking with another senator, and he nudges me, nodding at a miniskirt ahead of him. He shakes his head, grinning. *Quiff quiff quiff,* he murmurs. I laugh.

Noone is still in the big office. She said she would make selected calls to selected members of the press. Different men, different spins, she said. Not to worry. I leave her at her desk, her hair freshly combed, new makeup on her cheeks, two packages of cigarettes next to the telephone. Coins lie atop the cigarettes. She is excited, anxious for me to be gone so she can begin her telephoning. Straight-faced I say that I think I'll wait and listen to the first call, see how it goes. She shakes her head quickly, *No.* She would be inhibited with me on the extension phone. It is better if she does it alone. This is her job, she says. The reason she is paid twenty-eight thousand dollars a year.

"Twenty-eight, five," I say, and her humor returns.

"It's cheaper than a trip to Rome," she says.

I know her friends, so I know where to look tomorrow. I mean which newspapers, and which network. They will be very interested in this story because I am on all the short lists for vice-president. They will say this will take me out of the running, and they are right, although Noone will not believe it. I tell her she is crazy, she had better set her sights elsewhere. A Catholic separated from his wife, three children.

"I can live without the vice-presidency," I tell her.

"There are seven congressional districts in Iowa," she says, and begins dialing.

A Guide
to the Architecture of
Washington, D.C.

THE day after the election he took five of them through the Oval Office and all of the rooms in the West Wing. They were polite and attentive, but a little cold. Candler understood and didn't mind. He thought they looked very young and would improve with age; give them four years in the West Wing and they'd age quickly enough. Candler showed them everything, from the location of the coat closets to the safes and special communications equipment. He explained that many of the pictures on the wall were personal and would leave with the men who owned them. All of this was carefully taken down by the one with the notebook. There was no question that this new crowd would want a thorough housecleaning, which was entirely understandable. The old man told him to expect that and be courteous about it.

Candler filled them in as best he could on the way the White House was run. Who had which offices, and the lines of authority each to each. It was a pointless exercise, because the staff followed the whim of the top man, and no staff was like any other. But there were certain practical considerations, and Candler understood those after eight years. The six of them made desultory conversation for thirty minutes, then got up to leave.

"See you later," one of them said with a smile.

"Anytime," Candler replied.

He showed them to the door and watched them walk away down the asphalt drive. They looked like college boys in their tweed coats and careful manners. He knew one of them slightly, from a conversation they'd had before the election. The old man had told him to offer his services to solve a financial problem and he'd done that, only to be refused. No thanks, they'd said; we can handle it. We appreciate your interest, and your boss's; but no thanks. This was the new crowd, and they were very jealous about that. Also they were the new crowd running against the record of the old. Same political party, different generations.

Candler watched them go and felt no regrets. Eight years was long enough, and he was tired. His work was done. Candler thought he would go to Sun Valley for a month and arrange to be back in town just before the inauguration. He hadn't missed one of those in sixteen years. It signaled continuity, an orderly transition. Then he'd go back to New York and begin his book. And after that — time would tell.

The five men had walked down the asphalt and were now standing on the sidewalk in Pennsylvania Avenue, looking back at the White House. Measuring it for size, Candler thought; thinking about the offices. The offices in the basement, the ones on the second floor, and the *real* offices. The ones next to the Oval Office. He grinned, knowing *exactly* what they were thinking.

Then he turned and hurried back inside.

He listened to Billingsly's innocent drawl, the one that

had deceived two generations of lawyers. "Tell me again," Billingsly said. "What is Oldfield offering?"

"The usual guarantees. The front money, the fringes. For the usual services, and these are specified. It's a tight contract. I told them who I could bring in with me, and these are very, very good clients. Top-of-the-line people. But the thing is this. They won't talk about the other stuff. 'We'll take care of that when it comes up,' they said. Of course they want me to stay public. They don't want an invisible man."

"No."

"And that's all well and good, they're good people and all that. Except that the guarantee isn't all that high. It's high enough, but it's nothing exceptional."

"How high?"

". . . and they've been slipping lately. They were hurt when the judge died. To a certain extent, they're living on reputation."

"How high, Paul?"

"A hundred and a half, plus a percentage. Of course they're counting on me to deliver."

"Any problem there?"

"No, none. As I said, these people are top-of-the-line people." There was dead air between them, and Candler lit a cigarette. They had plenty of time, there was no hurry. Candler heard his friend breathing heavily into the telephone. He switched buttons to the squawk box, so he could talk from anywhere in the room. "None at all," Candler said.

"It's a good offer, Paul."

"Fair, not good."

"When I began it was eight dollars a week and you walked to court and all the fees went into the hands of the senior partners. But I was twenty-five then."

"And I'm forty-one."

"And I'm seventy." Billingsly paused. "What are your options?"

"Christ, I'd like to get back into the game. Tom, I'd give my left nut to get back into it. But there isn't any entry. They're all new people now. Hell, some of them I don't even know. The guy there that has my old job, Christ, he used to be the attorney general of Christ, *Idaho*, or some damn place. I don't even know their names, where they came from. New crowd entirely."

"I know what you mean. Same thing happens every time the big man dies or is defeated. They bring in the new brooms, but the last time we had this kind of situation was Coolidge and Hoover. I mean where there was an election, a definite stop and start. I remember what happened then. They —"

"Hell, we didn't have a *government* then. All we had was guys sitting in offices. Not a government, the way it is now." Candler lit a cigarette. "Well, back to the problem at hand. What do you think of Oldfield's offer?"

"He's your ticket of admission, Paul."

"What do you really think of it?"

"I think it's a pretty good offer. That firm's right for you just now. You've got to think long-range. Oldfield must be older than I am, and his kid is a horse's ass. The judge is dead, but they've got five or six others in there who know their way around. Damn well. It's still a quality outfit, and your going there could make a difference. The front money's not all that important in the last analysis. You know good and well that they can't get the sort of business you can, and that no one in that place has got your contacts. Just leave the contract open-ended. That's my free legal advice. Write it for a year, then renegotiate."

"Fisher got more," Candler said.

"Well, yes."

"More front money, and a guarantee he could move on damn near anything he wanted, anytime he wanted. He got carte blanche."

"Of a certain kind. But we've been through this before, and you've got to accept it. You've got to remember who Fisher was and what he did. And how he did it. The kind of exposure he had. You know the truth and I know the truth, but Fisher's new employers don't know it."

"Those were great days," Candler said.

"Screw the great days. This is right now."

"Well, Fisher got his name on the door. Davis, Davis and Fisher. The son of a bitch. I'm surprised he didn't make them reverse it. Fisher and Davis. Or maybe just Fisher and Partners."

"He's no novice at writing contracts."

Candler was silent for a moment. Then: "Maybe I ought to wait until the book is out."

"He was more visible than you. That was just the way it happened, nothing to do with you or with him. You were too damn stiff with the newsies, Paul. Fisher wasn't, and that made the difference. The *Time* cover, all that horseshit. Everybody thought after a while that Ted Fisher was running the government, when in reality it was you." The old man barked a laugh and they were silent again. Candler stared morosely at his drink. He switched off the squawk box and picked up the telephone receiver.

"Maybe if I wait until the book is out, maybe then . . ."

"Paul, the book is *now*. Your chips are *then*. The past in this case is more important than the present. Everybody is friendly as hell, but you've got to put yourself in their shoes. They're not buying an author, they're buying a lawyer. Historians are a dime a dozen, Presidents' lawyers aren't. Now I know it's a fine book. But what you're giving Oldfield is the past. That's what you've got on the table, that's your ante. You know where to go, he doesn't. You know the passwords, he doesn't. You know the graveyard, and he hasn't a clue. That's your little secret. You can win the Nobel Prize with that book and it won't matter a damn to Oldfield. Believe me that."

"The book will get attention."

"Yeah, attention will be paid. But you're not getting this job through the *New York Times*."

"So you're saying this to me: go now."

"Absolutely, unless you've got something better. The longer you wait, the more you've got to contend with memory. Memories fade. It's all on the instant now, and you've got to strike while you're hot. You've been with that book for two years, and you're already a former. Am I right? How do they identify you? Paul Candler, former special counsel to the President. Right? Am I right? And it's an ex-President."

"Right."

"So you have a problem."

"I guess I didn't tell you that I let out the word that I was available, if they wanted me."

"You did *what?*"

"Well, I did."

"Christ, Paul."

"It took about a week for the word to come back, through a third party. They said they'd like to talk about it sometime, but there was nothing just now in the White House. They wondered, though, if I'd consider chairing a . . . study group." Candler listened to Billingsly's impatient breathing. "This was to be a presidential commission to do with auto safety. Me and about four hundred other distinguished citizens. To find out for Mr. and Mrs. America if driving is good for you. You know, there'd be me and the president of some third-rate university, a sports hero, a defeated politician, some women, a writer down on his luck. A retired Supreme Court justice — hell, that could be *you* except you're not retired. But don't worry, I'll pass your name along. I'll tell them that Mr. Justice Billingsly is ready and willing —"

"Paul Paul Paul."

"All right, a mistake."

"For a smart guy, you sometimes do the damnedest things."

"But it's done now."

"Never never never never never."

"Right."

"I would have done that for you. I see them all the time. I mean I see quite a lot of them, including The Man. That's the sort of thing that has to be handled with great diplomacy, because they don't know what's behind it. Those midwesterners, they're suspicious as hell. It's the sort of thing where you deal face-to-face, after the initial contact.

I would have done that. Pleased to do it. Why didn't you ask me about it, before you went ahead? Look, some of them are top-notch people. It's a mistake to think they're all opportunists."

"Right right right."

"Are you serious? Did they really ask you to chair a study group?"

Candler thought he had been too flip, that he'd made himself unnecessarily vulnerable. But if he couldn't trust Billingsly, there was no one he could trust. "Yes, I'm serious about the study group. The President himself suggested it, they said. The President himself would be honored. Delighted. Very pleased. By the way, they call him 'The Man.'" Candler was silent, waiting for a reply. When there was none, he went on: "The Man wants this. The Man wants that. The Man says this. The Man believes."

"Yes, I know that."

"I was going to reply that I'd be pleased to do it. My experience in settling railroad strikes, negotiating with the Cubans, strong-arming the oil men — let alone that Canadian business — that eminently qualifies me. Rich experience, put to good use."

"Well, they think they've got an identity problem over there. They want to separate this administration from the last, and that's why there are so few holdovers. For better or worse, Paul, you're identified with the *ancien régime*. So am I, for the matter of that. But they can't do anything about me, I've got my job for life. I'm sorry to tell you this, but the book won't help. It'll just serve to reinforce their paranoia about . . . loyalties."

"But Tom, the old man's almost dead. How can you have loyalty to a dead man?"

"It's who you're identified with. That's your problem just now. And it won't go away, not until the second term at least and maybe never. Well, not *never*. But it's something you've got to face up to."

"Yeah, I suppose. I suppose." Candler put the squawk box on and went to the bar to mix himself a fresh drink. Talking with Billingsly depressed him. He said over his shoulder, "Well, Fisher seems thick enough with them."

"I suppose you know why."

"Unh."

"You *do* know why."

"I've heard," Candler said carefully.

"The meeting at the club."

"Right."

"Seven figures, Paul. And Fisher was the broker for that. Hell yes, he's in tight. You can't ignore that kind of help. And he spends a lot of time with the newsies, which doesn't hurt any. And it develops that he and The Man share a passion for . . . duck hunting."

"Oh Christ," Candler said.

Billingsly was silent for a moment. Then he added: "I hear on pretty good authority that he'll be offered Billy's job . . ."

"Deputy secretary of *defense?*"

"Right."

Candler stood at the bar, absently moving ice in his glass. He reached for the bottle of Scotch and filled the glass to the brim. He sighed. Forbearance. "When?"

"End of year."

"But I keep reading about a campaign for governor."

"No, that isn't going to happen. They took some polls and it showed up very badly; he's got a carpetbagger image. And as a matter of fact, he's a lousy politician. He knows that, and the talk about running for governor was a screen to keep his name out front. He wouldn't make a politician any more than you would."

"I don't know about that."

"I do. You and Fisher, you're inside men."

"You know a hell of a lot about what's going on, Tom. You sound like you're in pretty tight yourself." Candler paused, aware that he'd overstepped himself. "Sorry, Tom. I didn't mean that the way it sounded."

"No problem."

"It's just that Fisher irritates the hell out of me. I saw him a couple of weeks ago on the street. We went up to his office and had a drink. Biiiiig corner office, a carpet up to your eyeballs. Two telephones, a lot of soup-can art on the walls. And that one photograph on the desk, of the old man before he got sick. 'To Ted Fisher. Loyalist first last and always.' That was the inscription. Nice."

"Has Oldfield showed you around their place?"

"Yes. And to answer your question, my office there would be about a third the size of the one I had at the White House. Now that's a strange thing. A hundred and fifty thousand dollars a year guaranteed, and they give you an office the size of . . . an assistant to the deputy assistant undersecretary of . . . what? The Commerce Department. Some Daumier prints go with the office. It's got a view of another building, directly across the street. But if I strain

I can see the East River, at an angle, looking left out my window. It may be a mistake to go to New York with Oldfield, wouldn't it make a lot more sense to stay in Washington?"

"Fisher didn't."

"No."

"I think it makes more sense to broaden your base. And those New York lawyers. They're a little awed by Washington. They don't *know* it, not like we do, and they're a little afraid of it. They're afraid of it and patronizing about it, all at once. Oldfield's outfit is old-line, and they're probably being deliberately casual. But that'll stop when they have a serious problem and you can solve it for them. That'll stop right away at that time."

"New York's a pain in the ass."

"Well, you force yourself, Paul."

"A hundred and a half makes up for the discomfort."

Billingsly coughed and said casually, "Did Fisher talk to you at all about his plans? Did he say anything?"

"No. I got the idea he was going to make money for two or three years, then engineer a reentry. That's why I'm surprised at your news. But we're pretty cautious with each other, there's still some hard feeling. Not on my part, on his." Candler laughed a short, quick laugh. "Know anywhere I can scare up seven figures?"

"So he didn't say anything specific."

"Not to me."

"Well, wait it out."

"Sure. And I'll go to work for Oldfield, and we'll spend a lot of time reminiscing about the old man, and then he'll start to ask me the questions. 'What really went on at the meeting in Ottawa?' Or, 'Tell me the straight story behind the oil deal, did Big Clint really say what they said he said?' Or he'll buy me a big lunch at the Harvard Club and we'll have a drink or two and some fine wine and he'll say, just about the time the cigars come, 'Say Paul, I was talking to old X today and it turns out he's got a problem with import quotas.' Or with the FCC or the NLRB. Or someone from the White House is leaning on him and isn't there a way to do a quiet end-around? And I'll say, 'Don't worry, I'll look into it.' And I will, and maybe I can do something and maybe I can't, and the client won't be any the wiser and we can hike the fee a couple of hundred percent, and he can be a big man on the golf course back in Cleveland by saying he's hired Paul Candler to solve his Washington problem. Wink. Smile." He paused, listening to Billingsly's breathing. "Tom, I want to be where it's happening. I know what to do and how to do it. I had the place in the palm of my hand. I'm good at it, what I did for the old man. No one could come in cold and move a man around like I could. I couldn't put it in the book because the book is supposed to be about the old man, but it was *me* who sealed the oil thing. *I* negotiated. *I* set the terms. The old man gave me blanket authority, and I took it and the thing was settled to everyone's satisfaction. It never broke in the press, and it never will. I let Fisher and the rest of them massage the press, and they did a hell of a job. And got their names in the paper. Well, I've hinted at the oil deal in the book. Anyone who reads between the lines can guess at the truth of the matter." Candler heard Billingsly laugh. "Or part of the truth anyway."

"Yes, I was about to say."

"So now I'm out in the cold. Fisher's in, I'm out."

"Look at it this way. You'll make some dough for a couple of years. Then you'll come back in."

"The old man was some man to work for," Candler said. "Remember that look, the over-the-eyeglasses look? Just a glance across the desk. *Now you take care of this, and I want it done right.* Remember that, Tom? And we went off and did it and didn't bother him again until the thing was done. Just *did* it, with no questions asked. And no publicity either."

"Absolutely."

"I loved that old man."

"We all did. Do."

"That's where it is, you know. That's where it counts. Up against that, Oldfield and Wall Street are Dubuque." Candler took a long swallow of his drink and switched on the squawk box again. "But it's the old frontier now, that's for sure. And Fisher's playing bagman for the new crowd." Candler swirled ice around in his glass, standing at the bar with his back to the telephone. A habit he picked up in the West Wing, strolling around the office while he talked into the telephone.

"Paul? You know I never really thanked you for letting me see the galleys of the book. And agreeing to the changes. It would have been awkward as hell for me."

"I understand. I don't know how the passage got in there in the first place. It was careless research."

"Well, you know I appreciated it."

"Yes."

"Well, I guess that's it."

"All right, Tom. One last thing. I want to just pursue

this for a minute, if you've got the time. *What if* you took it up in a private way with your friends back there. Casually, no big production. You say to them, Paul Candler wants to get back into the government. He knows it's hard for you. But he'd like to work in the White House again. He thinks he can be useful to the President, and he's willing to take on damn near any assignment. Troubleshooting, speech-writing, anything . . ."

"It's a hard nut, Paul. What did you do about the auto safety thing?"

"Oldfield represents about half of Detroit, so I said I'd be delighted to take it on. When Oldfield heard about that, he was pleased as hell. That announcement won't be made for three or four months, so there's no problem either way. What do you think about talking to them? You can say you're not speaking with my explicit authority, necessarily, you're operating on assumptions. You can say I'm bored with life on the outside."

"I could do it all right," Billingsly said slowly.

"Well, good."

". . . except for the other thing. They *know* you're interested. You've brought your name to their attention. They know you're out there. I'd leave it to them now, and what I'll do is put in a word for you. I mean a very good word. Paul, they're hard as rocks right now."

"Well, hell. No hurry. We'll talk about it again soon."

"Right, we'll do that. Meantime, you think about Oldfield."

"You think definitely that I ought to take it?"

"I do. No question."

"In a couple of years, I ought to make half a million dollars."

"That's the spirit."

"Yeah. I'll buy some duck blinds." They were silent for a moment, the conversation almost at an end now.

"Take care, Paul."

"Give my regards to Fisher, if you see him before I do."

"You bet."

"And I ought to see you next month, when I get in town."

"Just let me know."

"And speak to The Man, next time you see him."

"You can count on it," Billingsly said.

Candler cradled the telephone and turned back to the bar. He remembered everything, and he knew his life wouldn't ever be the same; he knew Billingsly too well and understood all the nuances. He remembered the black Mercury sedans, with the telephones and the reading light in the rear seat. He was up every morning at seven sharp, swinging into the big circular lobby at a quarter to eight. He remembered the silence of the lobby, and the wan light from hidden lamps. In the early morning there were always one or two visitors seated on couches, nervous men waiting for appointments, who put down their newspapers when they saw him. It was as if they felt newspapers were an unnecessary frivolity, a sacrilege in his presence, something profane.

He remembered the two guards at the door and the old Negro receptionist at the desk near the far end of the room. There were different Negroes at different times, he could never keep them straight. He'd pause, it always seemed an eternity, then stride swiftly to the corridor that led to his own office: he felt the others watching him, following his progress. From the corners of his eyes he'd notice the old man at the desk struggle to his feet, looking at him with large watery eyes, and glide like a bird, soundless, to the corridor entrance. He'd wait there, ready to be of service — who knew if Candler had a message to be delivered, someone summoned, something fetched? Candler never did, and the old black man would then offer to take the briefcase for him. Candler'd shake his head, no; grimly, no. His fists tightened around the briefcase handles as he swung by the Negro with a nod and a muttered good-morning.

Then, safely inside the sanctum, he'd relax and stroll down the hallway to his office and the morning's business. Before he did anything he checked the appointment book to see what was scheduled. What was public, what private, and what personal. Then he checked the Oval Office to see if the old man was in. To see if there was anything special that day. Anything that needed doing. Anything at all.

It was the office, not the man. That was what the historians said, and for once the historians were right. Oh what a place Washington was, when you were there on the inside. Right in tight, near the Oval Office, where it happened. He'd been there for eight years, an assistant, a President's man. Now he was on the outs. He hated being on the outs more than he hated anything. For a President's man habit died hard, and suddenly he was afraid.

FINE WORKS OF FICTION
AVAILABLE IN QUALITY
PAPERBACK EDITIONS FROM
CARROLL & GRAF

- [ ] Asch, Sholem/THE APOSTLE — $10.95
- [ ] Asch, Sholem/MARY — $10.95
- [ ] Asch, Sholem/THE NAZARENE — $10.95
- [ ] Asch, Sholem/THREE CITIES — $10.50
- [ ] Ashley, Mike (ed.)/THE MAMMOTH BOOK OF SHORT HORROR NOVELS — $8.95
- [ ] Asimov, Isaac/THE MAMMOTH BOOK OF CLASSIC SCIENCE FICTION (1930s) — $8.95
- [ ] Asimov, Isaac et al/THE MAMMOTH BOOK OF GOLDEN AGE SCIENCE FICTION (1940) — $8.95
- [ ] Babel, Isaac/YOU MUST KNOW EVERYTHING — $8.95
- [ ] Balzac, Honore de/BEATRIX — $8.95
- [ ] Balzac, Honoré de/CESAR BIROTTEAU — $8.95
- [ ] Balzac, Honoré de/THE LILY OF THE VALLEY — $9.95
- [ ] Bellaman, Henry/KINGS ROW — $8.95
- [ ] Bernanos, George/DIARY OF A COUNTRY PRIEST — $7.95
- [ ] Brand, Christianna/GREEN FOR DANGER — $8.95
- [ ] Céline, Louis-Ferdinand/CASTLE TO CASTLE — $8.95
- [ ] Chekov, Anton/LATE BLOOMING FLOWERS — $8.95
- [ ] Conrad, Joseph/SEA STORIES — $8.95
- [ ] Conrad, Joseph & Ford Madox Ford/THE INHERITORS — $7.95
- [ ] Conrad, Joseph & Ford Madox Ford/ROMANCE — $8.95
- [ ] Coward, Noel/A WITHERED NOSEGAY — $8.95
- [ ] de Montherlant, Henry/THE GIRLS — $11.95
- [ ] Dos Passos, John/THREE SOLDIERS — $9.95
- [ ] Feuchtwanger, Lion/JEW SUSS — $8.95
- [ ] Feuchtwanger, Lion/THE OPPERMANNS — $8.95
- [ ] Fisher, R.L./THE PRINCE OF WHALES — $5.95
- [ ] Fitzgerald, Penelope/OFFSHORE — $7.95
- [ ] Fitzgerald, Penelope/INNOCENCE — $7.95
- [ ] Flaubert, Gustave/NOVEMBER — $7.95
- [ ] Fonseca, Rubem/HIGH ART — $7.95
- [ ] Fuchs, Daniel/SUMMER IN WILLIAMSBURG — $8.95

☐	Gold, Michael/JEWS WITHOUT MONEY	$7.95
☐	Greenberg & Waugh (eds.)/THE NEW ADVENTURES OF SHERLOCK HOLMES	$8.95
☐	Greene, Graham & Hugh/THE SPY'S BEDSIDE BOOK	$7.95
☐	Greenfeld, Josh/THE RETURN OF MR. HOLLYWOOD	$8.95
☐	Hamsun, Knut/MYSTERIES	$8.95
☐	Hardinge, George (ed.)/THE MAMMOTH BOOK OF MODERN CRIME STORIES	$8.95
☐	Hawkes, John/VIRGINIE: HER TWO LIVES	$7.95
☐	Higgins, George/TWO COMPLETE NOVELS	$9.95
☐	Hugo, Victor/NINETY-THREE	$8.95
☐	Huxley, Aldous/ANTIC HAY	$10.95
☐	Huxley, Aldous/EYELESS IN GAZA	$9.95
☐	Ibañez, Vincente Blasco/THE FOUR HORSEMEN OF THE APOCALYPSE	$8.95
☐	Jackson, Charles/THE LOST WEEKEND	$7.95
☐	James, Henry/GREAT SHORT NOVELS	$12.95
☐	Jones, Richard Glyn/THE MAMMOTH BOOK OF MURDER	$8.95
☐	Lewis, Norman/DAY OF THE FOX	$8.95
☐	Lowry, Malcolm/HEAR US O LORD FROM HEAVEN THY DWELLING PLACE	$9.95
☐	Lowry, Malcolm/ULTRAMARINE	$7.95
☐	Macaulay, Rose/CREWE TRAIN	$8.95
☐	Macaulay, Rose/KEEPING UP APPEARANCES	$8.95
☐	Macaulay, Rose/DANGEROUS AGES	$8.95
☐	Macaulay, Rose/THE TOWERS OF TREBIZOND	$8.95
☐	Mailer, Norman/BARBARY SHORE	$9.95
☐	Mauriac, François/THE DESERT OF LOVE	$6.95
☐	Mauriac, François/FLESH AND BLOOD	$8.95
☐	Mauriac, François/WOMAN OF THE PHARISEES	$8.95
☐	Mauriac, François/VIPER'S TANGLE	$8.95
☐	McElroy, Joseph/THE LETTER LEFT TO ME	$7.95
☐	McElroy, Joseph/LOOKOUT CARTRIDGE	$9.95
☐	McElroy, Joseph/PLUS	$8.95
☐	McElroy, Joseph/A SMUGGLER'S BIBLE	$9.50
☐	Moorcock, Michael/THE BROTHEL IN ROSENTRASSE	$6.95
☐	Munro, H.H./THE NOVELS AND PLAYS OF SAKI	$8.95

- [ ] Neider, Charles (ed.)/GREAT SHORT
STORIES $11.95
- [ ] Neider, Charles (ed.)/SHORT NOVELS OF THE
MASTERS $12.95
- [ ] O'Faolain, Julia/THE OBEDIENT WIFE $7.95
- [ ] O'Faolain, Julia/NO COUNTRY FOR YOUNG
MEN $8.95
- [ ] O'Faolain, Julia/WOMEN IN THE WALL $8.95
- [ ] Olinto, Antonio/THE WATER HOUSE $9.95
- [ ] Plievier, Theodore/STALINGRAD $8.95
- [ ] Pronzini & Greenberg (eds.)/THE MAMMOTH
BOOK OF PRIVATE EYE NOVELS $8.95
- [ ] Rechy, John/BODIES AND SOULS $8.95
- [ ] Rechy, John/MARILYN'S DAUGHTER $8.95
- [ ] Rhys, Jean/QUARTET $6.95
- [ ] Sand, George/MARIANNE $7.95
- [ ] Scott, Evelyn/THE WAVE $9.95
- [ ] Sigal, Clancy/GOING AWAY $9.95
- [ ] Singer, I.J./THE BROTHERS ASHKENAZI $9.95
- [ ] Taylor, Peter/IN THE MIRO DISTRICT $7.95
- [ ] Tolstoy, Leo/TALES OF COURAGE AND
CONFLICT $11.95
- [ ] van Thal, Herbert/THE MAMMOTH BOOK OF
GREAT DETECTIVE STORIES $8.95
- [ ] Wassermann, Jacob/CASPAR HAUSER $9.95
- [ ] Wassermann, Jabob/THE MAURIZIUS CASE $9.95
- [ ] Werfel, Franz/THE FORTY DAYS OF MUSA
DAGH $9.95
- [ ] Winwood, John/THE MAMMOTH BOOK OF
SPY THRILLERS $8.95

Available from fine bookstores everywhere or use this coupon for ordering.

Carroll & Graf Publishers, Inc., 260 Fifth Avenue, N.Y., N.Y. 10001

Please send me the books I have checked above. I am enclosing $_____ (please add $1.00 per title to cover postage and handling.) Send check or money order—no cash or C.O.D.'s please. N.Y. residents please add 8¼% sales tax.

Mr/Mrs/Ms _____

Address _____

City _____ State/Zip _____

Please allow four to six weeks for delivery.